Sandy
AND THE ROCK STAR

Books by Walt Morey

Angry Waters
Canyon Winter
Deep Trouble
Gentle Ben
Gloomy Gus
Home Is the North
Kävik the Wolf Dog
Operation Blue Bear
Run Far, Run Fast
Runaway Stallion
Scrub Dog of Alaska
Year of the Black Pony

Sandy
AND THE ROCK STAR

by Walt Morey

E. P. DUTTON   NEW YORK

Library of Congress Cataloging in Publication Data

Morey, Walter.   Sandy and the Rock Star

SUMMARY: Running away from his overly protective parents
and restricted life, a teenage singing star finds himself
on a remote island where he befriends a tame but frightened
cougar that he determines to protect from a vicious hunter.
[1. Pumas—Fiction.   2. Hunting—Fiction.
3. Islands—Fiction]   I. Title.
PZ7.M816San   1979   [Fic]   78-12375   ISBN: 0-525-38785-4

Published in the United States by E. P. Dutton,
2 Park Avenue, New York, N.Y. 10016,
a division of NAL Penguin Inc.

Editor: Ann Durell   Designer: Stacie Rogoff
Printed in the U.S.A.
10 9 8 7 6 5 4

Sandy
AND THE ROCK STAR

1

Alec Frost, the gamekeeper on Sportsman's Island, called the owner, George McKinzie, long distance. "You've been wanting to kill a cougar for more than two years. Well, I've found a cat I'm sure you'll like. This fellow is over eight feet long and weighs about two hundred and fifty pounds."

"Two hundred and fifty! That's a mighty big cat."

"My guess is at least two fifty. He's the biggest I've seen in more than twenty years hunting. This cat will make a fine trophy to add to your collection."

"That's what I want. A big trophy I can have mounted. Where'd you find him?"

"You've probably seen him. It's that movie and television cougar, Sandy."

"You mean the one that clawed up the actor who'd been teasing him a few weeks ago?"

"That's the one."

"But he's tame. I've seen pictures of him sitting in cars with models, even licking their faces. I don't want to shoot an animal that sits there and looks at me like a house cat, Frost. My friends would laugh me out of town. This has to be kept sport and all that, you know."

"This cat's not tame anymore, Mr. McKinzie. He's apparently gone ugly. Everybody's afraid to work with him now. The owner's not rich. He can't afford to keep him when he's not earning any money. He had to get rid of him. I bought him for you to hunt."

"I don't know," McKinzie said doubtfully. "I've seen that cat a lot of times on the tube. He looks pretty mild to me."

"Once a cat turns ugly, Mr. McKinzie, that's it," Frost explained. "Whatever he was before, he has now jumped his first man and downed him. He can't be trusted and he won't forget. Anyway, I'll go right to work on him as soon as he arrives on the island. I guarantee that when I'm through he'll be as wild as any cougar in the woods."

"Now you're talking sense. That's the way I want him," McKinzie said. "Wild and ugly. Can you make him ugly, Frost? It'll add zest to the game."

"I'll make him both wild and ugly, Mr. McKinzie. He'll be everything the wildest cougar is—maybe a little more."

"Good! Good!" McKinzie was getting excited at the prospect of hunting down and killing a vicious animal. "How long do you figure it'll take?"

4

"He should arrive here in a couple of days. I'll start immediately. Give me a week, ten days at most. I'll call you when I know he'll give you a good chase."

"That's fine. Just fine. I'll be waiting," McKinzie said and hung up.

Two days later the launch that brought supplies to the island from the mainland arrived with the cougar, Sandy, in a stout cage. The captain helped Alec Frost and Joe Ironwood, the Indian caretaker, wrestle the heavy crate onto the dock.

Frost walked around the cage carrying a rifle and looking in at the cat. "He sure is big," he observed. "Bigger than I thought he would be. Mr. McKinzie will be mighty pleased with this fellow."

The short, powerful Ironwood studied the animal and said nothing.

The crate was barely large enough to hold Sandy. His small, trim head with the butterfly patch of white hair under his delicate nose touched one end. His long black-tipped tail stuck out the opposite bars.

Frost raised the rifle and said, "All right, let's see what we've got here. Let him out, Joe."

"Hey!" The captain was startled. "You're not turning that cat loose!"

"That's what he was brought out here for," Frost said. "You know that."

"Of course I know. And I know about this cat, too. He's gone bad. He almost killed a man a couple of weeks ago. I don't figure to be a candidate for number two. You just wait a second till I'm gone.'' He got aboard the boat and headed back to sea.

"All right, Joe," Frost said. "Open the door."

Ironwood stepped forward, drew the bolts and swung the door wide.

Sandy was in no hurry. He calmly stood and looked out the door. Finally he dropped his head and leisurely, and with dignity, stepped outside. He yawned enormously and stretched his more than eight feet of sleek length. His big, needle-sharp claws, from which prey seldom escaped, ripped furrows in the dock planks as he tested their sharpness and strength.

Frost shifted the rifle and eased back the bolt. The cat looked even bigger outside the cage. From years of experience he knew how dangerous this animal could be. He was the biggest cat in North America. He had the strength to bring down an elk or a thousand-pound moose. One jerk of that big front paw could snap a deer's neck. He could strike with the speed of light and cover more than twenty feet in a single bound. Now he was doubly dangerous because he had been raised from a kitten in captivity and so did not fear humans. He had attacked his first man and found him easy prey. All his natural, wild cat instincts to kill, that had lain dormant during the years he'd lived with his trainer, could have come violently alive.

Sandy's eyes, nose and ears were hard at work. His delicate nostrils greedily sucked in all the ancient smells of this small island. There was the biting, fresh tang of the sea, the pungent aroma of pine and fir and of decaying and growing vegetation. His sharp ears were cataloging the near rumble of the surf, the silken whisper of wind through the trees, the cry of gulls lazily drifting on air currents overhead, and the raucous voice of a nearby crow. His yellow eyes looked at the sea, the inviting empty beach and the green wall of nearby trees. All these sights and sounds and smells meant freedom.

Frost suddenly realized that only Ironwood and he stood in the way of that freedom. He had made a mistake turning this animal loose so soon. He drew back the bolt on the rifle and waited.

The black tip of Sandy's tail curled lazily right, then left. He yawned again, exposing gleaming teeth; then he padded calmly up to Joe Ironwood, rubbed against his legs and began to purr.

Ironwood scratched at the base of his ears and Sandy lifted his head, closed his eyes and purred louder with sheer delight.

Ironwood laughed. "A tabby cat! A two-hundred-and-fifty-pound tabby cat. What do you know."

Frost scowled. "I figured for sure he'd turned mean and wild after jumping that actor. That's the nature of a cat. I don't get this. It ain't natural."

"It is for this fellow."

"Then our job's to make him wild—and mean, too. Mr. McKinzie will be mightly pleased if we can make this cat completely wild and meaner than sin." He tossed a length of rope to Ironwood. "Use this on him for a starter."

Ironwood tossed the rope back. "That's your job. I'll have no part of it."

"Don't tell me you're scared of him, Joe. And me standing right here with the rifle to protect you," Frost chided.

"I was hired as caretaker for the lodge, and to keep the trails around the island clear so Limpy McKinzie can play big game hunter when he comes out to shoot the animals he's imported. That's all I intend to do."

"You never have liked Mr. McKinzie," Frost accused. "You've been here six months and you still get that sour look every time an animal's brought in. You've got it now. If you hate it so much, why'd you come?"

"I needed a job bad. I didn't know the kind of place this was."

"There's nothing wrong with it. Lots of wealthy men have set up sporting lodges like this. Mr. McKinzie could afford it so he bought this island and built one. Before the accident that made his leg and hip so stiff, he'd ramble all over the world to hunt. He's no phony. I've seen his trophy room. It's great. Lions, tigers, grizzlies. You name 'em, he's got 'em. He was a great hunter."

"You mean butcher," Ironwood said dryly.

"What have you got against a man taking his sport the only way left to him?"

"There's about as much sport to this as if he shot the cat while he was still in the cage."

"You're crazy. This cat will have more than two

thousand acres of island with plenty of brush and timber to hide in.''

"All cut up with trails and lookout spots to make it easy for McKinzie, and him carrying a rifle that will shoot a mile and kill an elephant. The cat can't get off the island because it's ten miles to the mainland. Sooner or later McKinzie's going to kill him. If he's good and wild, and clever, too, and luckier than any of the other animals that have been brought out here, he might last an extra day or two. But in the end he's going to be killed.''

"So what else is this cougar good for? It pleasures McKinzie and gives you and me the best jobs we've ever had.''

"Then you take care of your job. I'm not that proud of mine.'' Ironwood patted Sandy between the ears and stalked off the dock.

Frost watched the Indian out of sight; then he doubled up the rope, walked to Sandy and brought it down across his back with all his strength.

Sandy squalled with pain and surprise. He bounded to the edge of the dock and stopped to look back. Frost had the rifle to his shoulder. There was a deafening explosion, and splinters sprayed into the air under the cat's nose, stinging his face. Frost's voice bellowed harshly, "Get out of here, cat. Beat it! Get! Get!''

A second shot showered Sandy's front legs and chest. He leaped off the dock into the brush and disappeared.

Few animals can equal a cougar's speed over a short distance, and Sandy was a streaking, tawny blur. He burst into a trail and raced along it, long tail streaming out behind. The trail split. He swerved into the right fork without slackening speed. His big, soft pads made not a whisper nor disturbed a single twig as he covered the ground in giant bounds.

The trail turned and twisted along the floor of a shallow ravine, punched through dense underbrush, skirted the edge of a field of tall grass and finally entered a grove of giant trees so thick they shut out the sun. Here the trail was soft and spongy, the air damp and rank with the scent of decaying vegetation. A thick layer of moss carpeted the forest floor, rocks, down trees and stumps. Well into the grove the trail abruptly ended at the edge of a small, clear glade. Sandy stopped, panting, to inspect it.

The glade was almost a perfect circle. It was overgrown with coarse, thick grass on which the sun lay warm and inviting. Across the glade a jagged column of bare rock punched castlelike out of the earth as high as the treetops.

Cats love high places, and this one held some interesting shelves and ledges. Also Sandy had been frightened, and it is the nature of the cougar to find some high place as a retreat. He trotted across and began to climb.

Climbing was easy for the big cat. He leaped lightly from rock to rock and ledge to ledge, and worked his way to the very top. There he stretched out on the table-flat pinnacle to catch his breath. In the distance white lines of surf marched steadily ashore. A flight of gulls went over, heading for the beach. Somewhere near, a pair of jays made a noisy racket in the brush. Directly below, the little glade lay sun-warmed and still.

For the first time in his life Sandy was in a strange world of sights and sounds and smells without his owner beside him talking quietly, leading him in the things he was supposed to do. Without that security he felt lost and uncertain.

His breathing had returned to normal when Frost came up the trail and entered the little glade. Sandy sat up, leisurely curled his long tail about his feet and looked down curiously. The man crossed to the foot of the rock pinnacle, lifted something to his shoulder, and again there came the thunderclap of sound that seemed to rip the day apart. A chunk of rock at Sandy's feet exploded, showering and stinging him. He whirled, bounded off the top and raced down the opposite side in breath-catching leaps. Another shot and harsh shouts followed him. For the first time he associated pain and fear with man.

He fled headlong, leaping rocks, stumps and logs. He burst into a trail and streaked along it. At a sharp turn he plunged back into the dense, rank-smelling un-dergrowth. He came abruptly to the sea and raced along the shore, staying carefully in the protection of long grass and brush. He sailed easily across a small stream, charged across a marshy area, sending black, muddy water flying. His heart was hammering and he was pant-ing again. Finally he quit the beach and entered dense timber once more. Here the wild panic gradually sub-sided. He dropped back to a brisk trot.

Sandy crossed and recrossed a network of trails. Sometimes he padded along one for a short distance, then faded into the brush only to reappear following another in a different direction. His delicate nostrils and sharp eyes were aware of a variety of small, strange game, and the natural silence of his movements brought him very close. Squirrels chattered angrily from tree branches. A small covey of birds sprang into the air almost under his nose with a frantic beating of wings. A pheasant exploded out of the grass and zoomed off through the trees, trailing a string of startled squawks. Rabbits were constantly scurrying off ahead of him. He was not hungry so he paid them little heed.

The sun was sliding low down the sky when he finally crept into a black hole under a fallen tree and lay down to rest. He stayed there until the sun fell into the sea and night spread in thickening layers over the earth. Fog banners lifted off the water and ghosted through the trees.

Night brought Sandy forth. It was the first time he'd ever been in a forest in the dark. He sat in front of the hole, curled his long tail around his feet and looked about. His nostrils were filled with the raw bite of the fog and the sea. The odor of the land was stronger and stronger. It was a wildness flowing out of strange, mysterious places. It touched a like wildness in Sandy that had been bred into his kind since time began. True to his breed it now came alive.

His stubby ears registered the sounds of the night waking. There was the soft rustle of small bodies moving through the grass and brush, the furtive scratching of tiny claws, the velvety beat of wings. From somewhere at sea a far-reaching call echoed again and again. Nearby a faint squeak heralded the death of a small animal as it was pounced upon by a predator.

Finally Sandy rose. The strongest of instincts in all animals began to waken—the homing instinct. He didn't know how far home was or the insurmountable obstacles that lay across his path. He only knew the direction, as sure as the migratory water fowl who fly the thousands of uncharted miles from the frigid Arctic to the balmy South each year for longer than man knows. Home was a small, warm house with a straw floor, a huge chunk of raw meat, and a human's gentle hands and soft voice.

He lifted his head as if taking direction from the faint breeze. Then he trotted off, his course as true as a compass setting.

It led Sandy unerringly to the little dock. He trotted to the very edge and looked across the restless sea. Across that dark water was the way to go. Sandy was an excellent swimmer but there was nothing solid in the distance to swim to. He paced back and forth, then finally trotted off the dock. He went back along the beach, hunting another way.

At a point that jutted into the sea, he waded belly-deep into the water and stood, eyes searching longingly. Finally he returned to the beach and delicately shook first one wet paw, then the other. Then he sat down, opened his mouth and for the first time in his life poured his loneliness into the night. It was a piercing, high-pitched sound likened by many to the scream of a terrified woman. It carried to the farthest reaches of the island. For a moment all night life was stilled. Twice more he gave vent to his loneliness and frustration. Then he quit the beach and faded into the dark beneath the trees at a moderate trot.

Many animals born and reared by man would starve if turned loose on such an island. Not so with Sandy. The cougar is strictly a flesh eater and is endowed from birth with the ability to hunt and provide for itself. Down through the ages the cat has stalked prey to live. Sandy was amply endowed to perform that task in the wild. He moved ghostlike on big, soft pads that sheated two-inch needle-sharp claws. His yellow eyes were particularly adapted for night prowling. Powerful muscles could launch his more than two hundred and fifty pounds with the speed and accuracy of an arrow. He had the ability to slip his big body through brush and grass without the slightest sound.

Sandy was hungry now and unconsciously he began to hunt. He followed a twisting trail until his delicate nose picked up a body scent. It led to a small clearing where a pair of rabbits were eating grass. He galloped toward them. In a flash they disappeared into the surrounding brush. Sandy trotted on. Soon he picked up another scent. This time he approached with all the ancient stealth of his breed.

A rabbit sat in the middle of the trail. Sandy slunk forward, belly flat, taking advantage of every bush and shadow. Twenty feet away he coiled powerful legs under him and waited with a cat's eternal patience. Finally the rabbit turned its head to snip off a grass stem. Sandy launched himself forward. The rabbit was not aware of the cat until it was too late.

The rabbit was the first thing Sandy had ever killed. He made short work of it and continued on. Later he caught and ate another and his hunger was satisfied. But it was night and he trotted on, exploring the island.

Sandy's wanderings finally brought him to the lodge nestled in a grove of trees. He padded completely around it, sampling the familiar man and building sights and smells. He was especially attracted to a small outbuilding because it was about the size and shape of the one in which he'd spent most of his life. He sniffed about the door, reared against it and rattled the metal hasp that held it closed.

A door in the lodge opened. A short, barrel-chested bow-legged man stepped quietly out. Sandy whirled to spring away; then the man spoke and his voice was soft and intimate, like his owner's. Sandy hesitated, belly flat to the ground, ears laid back and lips lifted in a half snarl.

"You've got to be quieter, friend," Ironwood said. "Alec Frost could hear you and he'd be right out with the rifle to scare the living daylights out of you. I see he's already begun."

Sandy still crouched, ready to spring away, but he listened to the Indian's gentle voice. "I heard you scream tonight. I know how you feel, but that's bad. Apache legend says that when the cougar screams somebody's going to die. Did you know that? I'm afraid you sounded your own death knell. You know, you and I could be good friends in no time. But that's the worst thing that could happen to you. You'd trust me. Then you'd begin trusting other men, like Alec Frost and Limpy McKinzie. That would be fatal. You've got to be wild as a marsh hare when old McKinzie comes to hunt you down. It won't do a bit of good. But it might keep you alive a few hours or a day longer. There's only one small thing I can do to help you now. That's to make you hate me, too." He bent and picked up a stick. "This is for your own good, Sandy. So long and take care." He hurled the stick with all his strength.

Sandy was gone in a bound.

Sandy continued to prowl the remainder of the dark hours, acquainting himself with the sights, smells, sounds and the shape and size of the island and its surrounding sea.

Near dawn a biting wind sprang up, bringing a fine driving rain. All the island's night life began hunting shelter. Sandy came again to the little glade and the black bulk of the rock pile. He remembered the high, flat top, the interesting crevices and ledges. He began to climb.

High up Sandy came to the dark entrance of a cave and entered. It was spacious and dry and out of the weather. The walls and ceiling reminded him of the interior of the house where he'd spent most of his life. From the entrance he could look down on the dripping world. It was a perfect place to rest and sleep.

That night set the pattern of the following days. Day after day and through the nights Sandy explored every part of the island as he searched for a way that would take him toward home. A map of the island and its intricate maze of trails, thickets and timber patches formed in his mind. He learned the spots where possum, raccoon, rabbits, squirrels and other small game abounded, and so he ate well.

Each night he was drawn irresistibly back to the little building at the lodge. He paced around it, sniffing the mouth-watering aromas that oozed through the crack of the door. Again and again he reared against it, trying to get inside. He still associated the building with home. Only once was he interrupted. The latch was particularly loose and he rattled it especially loud. The big front door at the lodge opened and Frost stepped out with the rifle over his arm. Sandy dropped to the ground in the shadows and lay perfectly still.

The bandy-legged little Indian came to the door and Frost said, "You hear that rattling around out there? Some animal or something. I've heard it a couple of times."

"I've heard it," Ironwood said. "Raccoon. He rattles the hasp on the door almost every night. I'll fix it tomorrow."

The next night the hasp was tightened. It still rattled, but not loud enough to be heard in the lodge.

Sandy saw the tall, thin Alec Frost almost every day, and often more than once. The meetings never varied. There were always harsh shouts followed by the crash of the rifle and bullets coming frightingly close before he could dodge out of sight. Wherever he went the specter of Frost and the rifle hung over him. Only at night could he move about freely, for the man was never abroad after dark. Sandy came to hate Frost even more than the actor who teased him. But because of the rifle he feared him, too.

Ten days passed and Sandy had not a single day's relief from Frost and the rifle. Then one fog-shrouded morning he rounded a sharp turn in the trail and came face to face with Frost but a few feet away. Both stopped in surprise.

For the first time Sandy did not bound instantly away. He crouched belly-flat to the ground. The black tip of his tail lashed angrily. His yellow eyes narrowed. There was his tormentor. He could reach him in a single bound. Never had he been this close. His lips lifted in a savage snarl. Every muscle tensed for the spring. The temptation was great. Then the rifle crashed and the familiar geyser of dirt and pebbles stung his face and the harsh voice howled at him, "Get out of here, cat! Get! Get!"

Sandy leaped into the brush and disappeared.

That night Alec Frost excitedly called George McKinzie. "You cat's ready," he said. "He's good and wild; ugly, too. Come and get him."

2

Something awoke Paul Winters. He lay quiet for several minutes, listening. Through the open window came excited young voices yelling and arguing. The racket annoyed him. They had chosen this quiet motel in Seattle so he could rest. He got out of bed and went to the window. Three floors below, a dozen or so boys were packed into a tight knot in a vacant lot behind the motel. They were choosing up sides to play softball.

Across the field, a couple of hundred feet away, a huge billboard displayed his picture. It showed a fifteen-year-old boy with a solid, bony frame that gave promise of a big man. His mouth was open, head thrown back. The shock of curly black hair fell with studied carelessness across one eye. His arms were wide open as he sang. Beneath the picture, foot-high words said: Paul Winters in Concert. The Sensational Singer. He'd seen the identical billboard in every city they'd visited on this tour. It always gave him the odd feeling someone was using his name and face.

The gang below broke apart. Half scattered loosely across the field. A boy began pitching to the batter. There was much shouted advice and good-natured heckling. The batter swung and popped out to the first baseman. Another took his place.

They were having a good time. Paul felt a sense of loss and frustration. He'd never done any of the things other kids his age did. His time was spent with adults in their world. What he'd give to play with a gang like this just once. All his life, it seemed, he'd been preparing for his big break as a singer.

When he rebelled at the constant practice and study, the endless rehearsals and auditions, his mother always said, "When your break comes, then there'll be plenty of time to relax and play and do the things you want."

And his father always added, "Remember, Paul, opportunity knocks but once. You've got to be ready for it. And you will be. Opportunities," he liked to say, "don't grow on trees like apples."

Three years ago the big break came. He hit. Now he had less time to himself than ever.

He understood his parents' obsession with his becoming a big singing star. For years they had dreamed of stardom. His mother was one of a girl trio that sang with a band. His father played a good trumpet. They were good, but not good enough. For them the breaks never came. The era of the big bands passed. There were hundreds of singers and trumpet players out of work.

Then Paul began to grow up. He had his mother's soft, pleasing voice; a natural, easy presence before an audience. And most important he loved to sing. Both parents recognized the possibilities. They bent every effort into building him into a star.

Three years ago the break came when they hired Henry Matthews for his manager. Matthews was a smart, intense, fat little man. He knew the music and promotional business. His only interest was making Paul a star. Paul's mother and Matthews were much alike. They completely agreed on anything that furthered Paul's career. His father also agreed, but he was not so intense as the other two.

"Wintertime" was especially written for Paul. With the hit song, a new star was born. Doors that had been closed miraculously opened. His parents were overjoyed. Through him they now lived the success that had escaped them. And they thought that after watching them for three years he hadn't figured that out? For pete's sake!

Paul didn't mind that they shared the spotlight with him. What bothered him more and more was that now his time was completely controlled. His parents and Mr. Matthews drove him harder than ever. He worked, worked every day. At all appearances he wore the clothes chosen for him, said what they told him to say, or stood silently by while Mr. Matthews and his parents did the talking. He was like a mechanical toy. They wound him up, pressed the button, pulled the strings. Paul opened his mouth and performed exactly as he'd been trained.

After three years as a star he felt he'd earned the right to be consulted on some things. He complained bitterly. There were people he couldn't work well with, auditoriums he didn't like, songs he felt weren't suited to him because he had no feel for them. But his parents always gave him the same old moth-eaten answer they'd used on him when he first started out. "You're just a boy. You don't know what's good for you. We do. Your time will come—but not yet." For pete's sake, did they think he hadn't learned anything the past three years?

Down below a batter sent a long fly ball sailing over the second baseman's head. There was shouting and running. The batter slid into first on his stomach—safe. Paul glanced at the bedside clock. Half past two. His parents and Henry Matthews were at the auditorium, seeing to last-minute arrangements. There was at least an hour and a half before they'd return and he wasn't tired or sleepy. On impulse he crawled out the window, went along the balcony and descended the fire escape to the ground.

He was standing to one side watching when the catcher yelled, "Hey, you want to play?"

"Me?" Paul asked, surprised.

"Yeah, you. We're short a man. You can play out there." He pointed. "Center field."

Paul hesitated.

"Hurry up," the catcher yelled. "Batter's up."

Paul trotted out to the designated spot. A blond boy playing on his left came over and said, "Watch this guy. He can knock the cover off the ball."

"Sure," Paul said.

The game resumed. The batter swung and swung. On the third strike he popped up to the pitcher. The next fanned. The runner going from second to third was thrown out. The side was retired.

A redheaded boy struck out. The blond who'd played in the field with Paul got a single. Paul was at bat. He was nervous. He had never struck at a pitched ball in any kind of game. Twice he swung mightily and missed. The last strike connected solidly and the ball sailed into the field.

He dropped the bat and sprinted for first. The kids were yelling like mad. He pulled up at first and they shouted, "Go on! Go on!" He dug out for second. Halfway there they began howling, "Slide! Slide!" From the corner of his eye he glimpsed the ball coming in from the outfield. He dove headfirst on his stomach, reaching for the board that served as a base. He hit it in a cloud of dust. He was safe. He managed to steal third but again he had to slide. On a pop fly he crossed home plate. A run! His teammates pounded him on the back and cheered. He had never felt better.

A couple of innings later he got another hit. He threw a man out, caught a fly and then popped out himself.

They never did finish the game. Somebody suggested

they stop for hamburgers, and they gathered about and pooled their money. They were a dollar short, but Paul made up the difference and a couple of them went off to a nearby stand. When they came back, both teams lounged about on the ground and ate and talked.

"We've got to meet here tomorrow and finish this game," the blond who'd played in the field with Paul said.

"Why not," a boy named Bud on the other team agreed. "We were just getting the feel of it. We'll wipe up the ground with you guys tomorrow."

"You didn't today. You won't tomorrow," somebody else put in.

"The game wasn't over," Bud said. "We would have. Hey, how many can come?"

The catcher on Paul's team couldn't. He was going fishing with his father on the Skagit River. Another was going to an uncle's farm to work for a couple of weeks. That ended the game talk and led to a general discussion of what they were doing, or had planned, for the rest of the summer. A couple, whose fathers owned fishing boats, were going aboard to work. They had exciting tales of seining salmon and seeing whales and sharks and riding out storms. Four others were planning a fifty-mile hike through virgin wilderness along the Skyline Trail.

"You're going alone?" Paul asked.

"Sure," Bud said. "We did it last year."

"But you can't hike fifty miles in one day," Paul

said. "Where do you stay at night and where do you eat?"

"We pack our own grub and cook right out on the trail. Sleep in our sleeping bags on the trail, too."

"Right out in the open? On the ground?"

"Sure. Man, is that something. You just lie on your back up there, watch the clouds go by and sleep under the stars, and the silence is miles deep."

"We almost got chased by a bear last year," another offered.

"What about getting lost?" Paul asked.

"Not much chance," Bud said. "The trail's marked and everything. My dad'll meet us at the end with the car."

"Your folks don't worry?"

"Nothing to worry about," Bud said. "Our folks know we can take care of ourselves."

Most of them were doing something. Fishing, hiking, working somewhere, even picking beans and berries in local fields. The blond boy had been watching Paul and now he asked, "You said your name was Paul. Paul what?"

"Winters."

"Winters, sounds familiar. Seems like I've seen you before."

"Winters, Paul Winters," another said. His eyes lit on the billboard at the end of the field. "Hey! you ain't that Paul Winters!" He looked from the billboard picture to Paul. "Oh, by golly you are!" His voice

25

climbed. "Hey, you guys, look who we've been playing ball with." He pointed at the billboard, "Him, that Paul Winters, the singer. How about that!"

They were all talking excitedly at once. "Hey, boy, what do you know! Wow!"

"What's it like singing?" one wanted to know. "I mean, walking out there in front of all those people? Man, I'd be petrified."

"Me, too. I wouldn't be able to open my mouth."

"Oh, you'd open your mouth all right. But what came out wouldn't sound like Paul."

"You get used to it," Paul said.

"No kidding? You're not scared or anything at all?"

"A little," Paul confessed. "But that's good. You should be a little scared. It makes you try harder. You know you've got to give a good performance, so you do."

"The money you make. It must take a truck to haul it away."

"I don't see any of it. My parents and my manager take care of that."

"No kidding. You even got a manager?"

"You have to have a manager."

"I guess you must go about all over, huh?"

"We're going to sixteen cities on this tour," Paul explained.

"You make records, too. I've heard some."

"I'll cut some more as soon as the tour's over. Then I'll do some TV guest appearances," Paul said.

"We can see you on TV, huh? I'll sure look for that."

"I'd like to hear you tonight."

"Would you all like to come?" Paul looked around at their eager, excited faces.

"Would we? Boy, would we!" they chorused.

"Okay." Paul felt warm and expansive. For the first time in his life he felt really important on his own. There were always a couple of hundred complimentary tickets. Mr. Matthews could give a dozen of them to his friends. "I'll get you all tickets."

He'd forgotten the time until he glanced up and there were his parents almost running across the field.

"Paul!" His mother's voice was shrill and angry. "What on earth are you doing down here? You're supposed to be resting."

"I wasn't sleepy," Paul said.

"You gave us an awful scare," she ran on, her voice sharp and accusing. "We got back from the auditorium and you were gone. We were about to call the police when I glanced out the window and saw you."

His father hauled him to his feet. "You all right? You're not hurt?"

"Of course not. I'm fine," Paul said. "The boys were down here playing ball and I came down and they let me play. Dad, I want tickets for the whole gang. . . ."

"You're going back to your room right now." His mother was taking charge again as always. "Come

27

along right now. We've got to get you cleaned up before someone sees you. You're a mess. Why, if people saw you looking like this . . .'' She shook her head, aghast at the thought. "Don't you ever do such a thing again."

Paul scarcely heard. He was looking at the faces of the gang. Where they'd been eager, surprised, envious, even worshipful a moment ago, there was now disappointment, amazement. The blond boy had a kind of pitying smile on his lips.

As his parents hurried him away across the field, there wasn't a sound from the group of stunned boys.

They rushed him up the back stairs so no one would see him. Once in the room his mother began scolding shrilly, "How could you be so thoughtless? You, of all people should know better. You know how important this tour is to all of us. Yet you risked everything, everything mind you, just to play a stupid game of ball with a bunch of—of I don't know what."

"There's nothing wrong with them," Paul said angrily. "They're a good gang."

"I'm sure they are," his father said. "But look at it our way, Paul. Your mother and Mr. Matthews and I have worked hard to build an image." His father always took the calm, reasoning approach. "You risked an awful chance of being seen this afternoon."

"What harm would it do for somebody to see me playing a little ball?" Paul demanded.

"Suppose some newspaper photographer saw you, and believe me they'd love nothing better. One picture of you the way you look now could ruin everything."

His mother hauled him in front of a mirror. "Look at yourself," she commanded angrily. "What if a picture of you like this appeared in the paper."

His face was streaked with dirt and sweat. His pants and shirt were torn. His black hair, with the gallant wave that his mother cultivated so carefully, falling over his eyes, stood on end and was several shades lighter with dust. In fact, he thought with a touch of pride, he looked dirtier than any of the other kids. He looked like he'd played a hard game, and he had. He'd got two solid base hits and hadn't fanned once. He was proud of his looks.

"Do you realize," his mother ranted as she did so often, "how many thousand dollars could be forfeited if you missed the concert tonight?"

"I'm not going to miss it," Paul shot back. "You sound like this won't wash off. It's just plain dirt. But even if I missed the concert it could be rescheduled. Nobody would lose anything."

"I'm talking about the people involved—musicians, sound men, stagehands, ushers." She didn't care about them. That was just an argument she used on him.

"They'd all get paid when the concert was rescheduled. But don't worry. I won't miss it."

"That's right, you won't," she snapped. "You've never missed one for something careless like this. You're not going to start now. You get in there and take a hot bath and wash that hair. Fred"—to his father—"call the desk and see if they have a house physician and get him up here."

29

"What do I need a doctor for? For gosh sakes," Paul said. "All I did was play a little softball. You're making a big thing out of nothing."

"Maybe one of those boys had a cold or something else. There's no telling what kind of bug you might pick up with a gang like that. Then you couldn't sing. Those scratches on your knees could become infected. With those other boys a little cold or infection wouldn't matter. They're tough. You're not like them."

"I could be with half a chance," Paul said.

"You can never be," his mother said emphatically. "Can't you get that through your head? You're Paul Winters, the boy with the golden voice, who can pack an auditorium with thousands of fans to hear him sing. You must always remember that."

He'd heard this lecture a hundred times. He wanted to yell at her and his father, "I got two hits today and one was a double that brought in a run. That's important to me, too. I want the same thing those kids have—a chance to be myself and have some fun. I've earned the right to have some say in my life."

Paul didn't say it. What was the use. They'd just tell him that he had no appreciation for all they were doing for him. He stalked angrily into the bathroom and slammed the door.

When Paul finally came out, a stocky, gray-haired man was waiting. His mother said, "Paul, this is Doctor Robbins."

"There's nothing wrong with me," Paul said. "I played a little softball, that's all."

The doctor smiled. "We'll just take a look."

He daubed disinfectant on the scratches, then went through the regular routine that Paul had endured countless times. After a few minutes he said, "Mr. and Mrs. Winters, there isn't a thing wrong with this boy. He's a very healthy specimen."

"He should be," Paul's father said, "he works out regularly in a gym three times a week, swimming mostly, and running. Under expert supervision of course."

"Of course," Dr. Robbins said.

"One of those boys might have had a cold or something and Paul could pick up the bug," his mother worried. "Paul can't have a cold, doctor."

"I understand," Dr. Robbins said. "I wouldn't worry about it, not this time of year."

"Paul is different," his mother persisted. "He's an entertainer, a singer, you know. The smallest cold could cause him to miss a concert. He simply can't do that."

"I know all about him." Dr. Robbins smiled. "My daughter has all his records and a front row seat for tonight. I'm sure you have nothing to worry about."

After the doctor left his mother said, "You must be worn out after all that playing."

"I'm not tired," Paul said sulkily. "I feel fine."

She went on as if she hadn't heard. "You must be absolutely fresh and rested tonight."

"I know," he said impatiently. "I know."

"It's going to be a big crowd. The auditorium is sold out. There's still an hour before you have to start getting ready. Why don't you take a nap. I'll wake you. Your father and I are going to relax a little ourselves down by the pool. If you need anything pick up the phone and call poolside.''

"All right," Paul said. "All right."

As they closed the door his mother said, "Have you noticed Paul seems to be getting more stubborn lately?"

"Well," his father answered, "he is growing up. You can't expect him to like being treated like a child."

Paul lay on the bed. He stared at the ceiling and thought about the game. His first game and he'd more than held his own with every boy there, he thought proudly. The solid smack of the bat hitting the ball felt good. The yelling kids urging him on gave him a warm, satisfied thrill such as his greatest stage success could not equal.

He thought of those kids, the things some of them had done, the places they'd been—and on their own. That was the big thing. He was older than several of them, but the only thing he'd ever done was walk out on a stage where every gesture, every move, every word was endlessly rehearsed and managed by adults.

He rose and looked out the window. The lot was empty. The gang had scattered to other interests. What did they call it? Doing your own thing. He'd never done his own thing. His father had told his mother she couldn't expect him to like being treated like a child. But she would never admit he was growing up.

He could still visualize the faces of the kids, shocked at the way she'd talked to him and led him off the field.

As if he was a five-year-old, he thought angrily. For a few minutes he'd been an equal with that gang of boys; then she had brutally destroyed him. And it had to stop. It had to stop now!

But what could he do that would shock them into realizing he was no longer a child? Hike the Skyline Trail with Bud, sleep out under the stars, go fishing aboard a boat, work on a ranch? Any of those things would do it.

A thought drifted into his mind like an airborne seed. He rejected it immediately. It came again. He took a restless turn around the room. The seed took root and grew. It became logical.

Suppose he took off, went somewhere, anywhere, just so he was alone, looking out for himself, making his own decisions. He could be gone, say a week, and never let them know where he was. That would certainly be a real shocker. It was one thing that would work.

The idea was so startling that at first he was afraid to accept it. It would be putting his parents through too much worry. And what about the concert tonight?

The concert could be postponed. Twice in the past that had been done at a moment's notice. Once when he got the flu, the other when a storm grounded the plane. As for his parents worrying, he could call them from somewhere and explain that he was all right and would return in a few days. But he'd not tell them where he was. When he did return, on his own, they'd know then that he was a self-sufficient young man who could look

33

out for himself and must be consulted on some of the decisions being made.

The hour was almost up. If he was going to do this he had to hurry. He wiped his mind clear of all further thought, for fear he'd lose his nerve, and began frantically dressing. Then he thought of money. His last dollar had gone to help buy hamburgers. His mother's purse was on the table. For the first time in his life he went into it. It yielded two hundred dollars. He took it all.

He was ready to go when he thought about leaving a note so they wouldn't worry too much. He found a pencil and piece of paper and began to write. *Don't worry. I'll be all right. This is something I have to do.* He thought a minute, then decided to add: They can postpone the concert until I get back. He had just written *They can* when the doorknob rattled and a key was inserted in the lock. They had returned before the hour was up. He dropped the pencil, ran to the window, climbed through onto the balcony and went down the fire escape. He sprinted down the street, rounded the corner and dodged into the alley. He kept running, going straight away from the motel.

Back at the door to his room an annoyed man continued trying to turn the key in the lock. Finally he glanced up at the number on the door, muttered, "Oh oh, this isn't 44," then went off down the hall.

3

At the end of the second block, Paul turned into the street. He quit running so as not to attract attention. He walked fast, head down, feeling he was losing himself in the heavy pedestrian traffic. A block later he came face to face with a three-foot square picture of himself in a store window. In the picture he wore almost the same clothing he had on now. He had to get rid of these clothes in a hurry and find a cap or something to cover his shock of black hair. He was surprised he hadn't been recognized already.

At the next corner Paul turned off the street and headed for a less thickly trafficked part of the city. Gradually the people thinned out. Within a half-dozen blocks he was in an older section made up mostly of old secondhand stores with dusty windows and dingy, dark interiors. He discarded his coat and tie in an alley, mussed his hair and returned to the street.

Paul decided against buying a complete change of

clothing in one store. Someone might think it strange and begin asking questions or take a good look at him.

In the first store he bought a lightweight, waterproof jacket. A block further on he found a cap that hid his shock of hair, and if he pulled it down a little, part of his upper face. Further on he bought heavy shoes, then jeans and a shirt. He changed clothes in a vacant stairwell in an alley and stuffed the rest of his suit in a garbage can. Back on the street he surveyed himself in a store window. He looked like any other fifteen-year-old who was just rambling around doing nothing during the summer.

Paul had a hundred and sixty dollars left. Not enough to take him a long way, but enough to lose himself for a few days. That should be time enough to convince his parents that he was old enough and big enough that what he thought and wanted should be reckoned with. Wherever he stopped tonight, he'd call and explain why he left. Now he had to decide where to go. He had to get out of the city in a hurry. By now his parents knew he was gone and had spread the alarm. Every police officer in the city would be on the lookout for him. Hitchhiking was out. It was against the law in this state. The first cop that saw him standing beside the road with his thumb out would pick him up.

The logical thing was to go somewhere by bus. He began to look for a bus station.

A police car cruised toward him. Paul turned his back and pretended to be looking at a window display. The car passed and rounded the corner. He began to walk fast. A couple of blocks later he almost ran into another police car. He started to cross the street and it was waiting in front of him for the light to change. He hesitated, then ducked his head and hurried across in front of it. The officer glanced at him, then returned his eyes to the traffic light. At the end of the next block he saw the bus depot sign.

The depot was small. There were only two clerks and a dozen old wooden benches. Six other people were waiting. Good. The police would likely be watching the big depots.

Paul studied a map tacked to a bulletin board and tried to decide where to go. He was from Arizona and a route that followed the ocean appealed to him. So did the name of a small town, Cove. It was right on the beach about fifty miles away. He went to the ticket counter and said, "One way to Cove."

The man punched out the ticket and said, "You've got about an hour's wait."

Paul sat on a bench and watched the slow hands of the wall clock snip away the minutes. A half hour passed. It was five-thirty. No one came into the depot. The ticket man was reading a paper. The second man disappeared into a back room. Paul was beginning to relax when two police officers came through the door. They stood just inside, close together, surveying the room. One went to the ticket counter and began talking with the man there. The other stayed near the door.

Paul came violently alert to danger. Why had the second man disappeared into the back room? To call the police? Why was that one policeman staying so close to the door? What was the ticket man telling the second officer?

Paul glanced quickly about the room. Past the officer at the door was the only way out. His whole scheme could end ingloriously right here before it ever got started. He hunched his shoulders inside the jacket, planted his feet firmly on the floor and waited. Every muscle was tensed to spring. He waited for the ticket man to point at him, the officer to turn and look directly at him, the one by the door to start toward him. The moment either man took a step in his direction he meant to leap, try to dodge him and get out the door.

Finally the officer at the ticket counter returned to his partner and the two left. Paul relaxed again.

The next half hour took forever to pass. Finally an old bus rattled up outside. The ticket man called out the towns. Cove was one of them.

The bus was about half full. Paul chose a seat toward the back. The driver hung about inside talking with the ticket man. Finally he came out, closed the door, and the bus pulled out.

Gradually the city thinned out. Open country began to appear. The road narrowed to two lanes that hunted its way between towering fir-clad mountains. It followed the sea so closely that at times they were almost on the beach. The bus stopped often and passengers got off and on. They passed through small settlements that squatted almost in the water. There were boats everywhere. Some were moored to docks, others cruised at sea. He remembered the salmon-fishing season was in full swing.

The sun dropped behind the mountains. The fleets of fishing boats were heading in when the bus finally stopped at a settlement. The driver said, "Cove, folks, end of the line."

Paul got off with the rest. He zipped up his jacket against the fresh bite of the sea less than a hundred feet away and looked for a motel. There was none.

Cove consisted of a dozen or so houses, a couple of small docks lined with fishing boats, two stores, a gas station and one small restaurant. He looked for a telephone booth. There was no booth. Maybe the restaurant would have one. He went in, climbed on a stool next to a red-faced old man who was drinking coffee, and ordered a hamburger and glass of milk. A telephone hung on the wall behind the counter, but everyone would hear what he said. He asked the waitress, "Are there any motels or places to stay here?"

The waitress shook her head. "A motel would go broke. Nobody stops at a little jerkwater place like this overnight. You looking for a room? Mrs. Ryan would maybe take you in."

"I was just curious." He'd have to be more careful of his questions.

His hamburger and milk came. He began to eat. In back someone put a coin in a jukebox and music filled the room. It was his first big hit. "Wintertime." He listened to his own voice extolling the wonders of snow, skiing and skating, frost on the windows, the Christmas-card look of the winter world. He thought, as he had so often, that the steel guitar was a little too loud. The music should have built a little more to the finish.

Beside him the old man jerked his head toward the music. "He does pretty good, huh?"

"I guess so." Paul paid strict attention to his eating.

"You guess so!" The old man was indignant. "I know so. Why, I've heard, what's his name, sing that song a hundred times, I guess.

"What's his name is Paul Winters, Carl," the waitress said.

"Hear he's just a kid," Carl rambled on. "Seen his picture in a paper once. Couldn't tell much how he looked. Some fool had put his big foot right in the middle of it."

"He looks something like this kid." The waitress jerked a thumb at Paul.

Paul crammed the last of the hamburger in his mouth, gulped down his milk, paid the waitress and left.

Outside he tried to plan what to do. The call to his parents would have to wait until he found a public telephone somewhere tomorrow.

The sun had dropped behind the hills. Night moved down the slopes and across the sea with surprising suddenness. He had to find a place to sleep. He walked down the road, around a sharp bend, and there facing him almost on the beach was an old vacant shed. He crossed the sand and grass to it.

The door was gone. The glass was broken out of the

single window. It was dark inside. In the middle of the one big room he made out a boat turned upside down resting on blocks. A pile of canvas and sacks lay nearby. He used them to make a bed under the boat and crawled under. He lay looking up at the black interior of the boat, listening to the endless pound of the surf. This wasn't anything like Bud's looking up at the sky and watching the clouds go by, or sleeping in the silence on the Skyline Trail. But he was alone, on his own, and this was anything but a comfortable hotel bed.

Paul wondered what his parents and Henry Matthews were doing. Probably hounding the police for news and being interviewed endlessly by the press. Leave it to Mr. Matthews and his mother to get all the publicity possible out of this. On that thought he finally slept.

It was daylight when he awoke. He stood in the doorway and looked at the new day. Fog tendrils drifted against the ragged face of the mountains. The sun was not yet up and the chill night wind blew steadily against him. At sea, fishing boats were moving through the misty dawn, motors muffled by the pounding surf.

Paul was hungry. He headed back around the bend to the little restaurant. It was open and there was a man behind the counter. He climbed on a stool and ordered ham and eggs, toast and milk. When he finished he paid his bill and asked, "When is the next bus?"

"Going which way?" the man asked.

Paul pointed, "Down the coast."

"One went through an hour ago. Next one is due about one o'clock."

Paul went outside. He was debating what to do when he saw the newspaper dispenser fastened to the side of the building. Through the glass the headline jumped at him. SINGING STAR MISSING. He got a paper, walked up the road, sat on a rock and read it.

His picture was beneath the headline. The story explained how his parents returned to the room and found him gone. The window was open and two hundred dollars was missing from his mother's purse. Much was made of the beginning of the note he'd written and hadn't finished and the softball game. It was suggested that he might have been seen, recognized, and there was foul play. The note ending with *They can* led the writer to believe that he might have been trying to leave some sort of message, again the hint of foul play. His mother was convinced that the note and missing money was a sure sign he'd been kidnapped.

"Paul," she insisted, "would never do such a thing. He had his own money. Besides," she pointed out, "he had absolutely no reason to leave. Look who he was. He was most happy being a singing star. He would never willingly run out on a concert and disappoint thousands of people. He was forced."

The police were checking the kidnap theory and requested they be notified if anyone saw a boy answering the following description. It was all there in a box—height, weight, color of eyes, hair, age.

He hadn't dreamed there'd be a kidnapping scare. But he should have known his mother would jump to the worst possible conclusion. At the first opportunity he'd call and tell her why he left, then hang up before she could start yelling and ordering him back or sending the police looking for him. The next town would surely have a phone. He folded the paper, stuffed it behind the rock and set off down the road.

Paul kept a sharp lookout for traffic. The double spotlights on top of a police car sent him scurrying into the brush. So did a small bus. He was surprised how many official-looking cars had amber lights on the roof that made them resemble police cars.

Near noon Paul topped a rise, and a pickup driven by a boy about his own age was upon him before there was time to duck out of sight. The pickup stopped beside him and the boy grinned out the window. "Want a ride?"

Because it was another boy, Paul said, "Sure," and got in.

The boy got the pickup going and asked, "How far?"

"The next town."

"Chinook," the boy said.

"That's right. Is it far?"

"About thirty miles. There's a couple of little places in between but they're just docks and boats and a few houses. I can take you about eight miles. I'm going fishing."

"I guess a lot of people around here fish."

"That's how most of us make our living. The salmon are running so we're all busy fishing."

A few minutes later the boy pulled up at the entrance to a lane. "This is where I turn off."

Paul got out and said, "Thanks for the lift."

"Sure." The boy waved and drove off.

An hour's hiking brought Paul to the first of the little settlements. It consisted of a store and gas station and a couple of houses. There was no telephone booth. Through the store window he saw a middle-aged woman behind the counter. He went in and bought a pound of wieners and a half-dozen buns. He hiked up the road, turned into the brush, found a stump and sat down and ate. When he finished there were three wieners and two buns left. He put the wieners in the bun package, stuffed it into his pocket and returned to the road.

Paul hiked along the shoulder of the road most of the afternoon, keeping a wary eye out for highway patrol cars. Several times he was offered rides. Each time he sized up the driver quickly and said, "No, thanks, I'm just going a little way." Two were older men who might start asking questions. The third was a sharp salesman type who might already be suspicious.

He became hungry again and finished the wieners and buns as he hiked. The sun was dropping into a blood-red sea when an older woman offered him a lift and he accepted. She took him right into Chinook and let him out in front of a restaurant.

Chinook was one block of stores, a couple of restaurants, two gas stations, and a motel at each end of the block. It was within a hundred yards or so of the beach. Unlike the other small towns, there was not the usual dock packed with fishing boats. Far up the beach he made out one small dock with a single boat tied to its face.

He was hungry again and tonight he wanted a shower and a soft bed in a room. And he absolutely had to find a phone to call his parents; a motel room would have one.

He had a hot sandwich and glass of milk in the restaurant, and returned to the street to study the two motels. They looked about the same size. One was newer than the other. He walked down to the new one and looked through the office window. He guessed the man behind the desk was in his forties. There was a rack of magazines and newspapers in the office. He had probably seen the paper and read the article about Paul.

He went up the block to the second motel. The man there was white-haired and wore glasses. There were no magazines or papers in sight. The chances were very good that this old man had not seen the article, and if he had, paid very little attention to a story of a missing boy singer.

Paul went in.

The old man looked at him over the tops of his glasses. Paul said, "I'd like a room."

"A room." The old man adjusted his glasses and looked closer at him. "You mean for yourself?"

45

"Yes."

"Where's your folks?"

"I'm alone." Then he added hastily, "For tonight."

"Oh, you're alone for tonight and you want a room.
Can you pay for it?"

"Yes." Paul took out his billfold.

The old man bent across the desk. "Where'd you say
you were from?"

"Off a ways," Paul waved vaguely. "I'm going
home."

"Off a ways. Would that be, say about eight miles?"

Paul nodded, "About that."

The old man straightened. "You wouldn't be from
that correctional school, Valley View?"

Warning raced through Paul. He began backing toward the door. "I don't know about any correctional
school. You can forget about the room."

"I intend to. But I'm not forgetting you, boy." The
old man was around the desk with surprising speed and
grabbed his arm in a viselike grip.

Paul struggled to jerk loose. The old man was surprisingly strong. He dragged Paul around the desk to the
phone, held him with one arm and started to dial. "I
know plenty about kids like you," he said angrily.
"Running off from that school all the time. You ain't
the first one I've caught."

Paul yanked and struck at the old man's face with his
fist but it did no good. The old man ducked his head
aside and kept dialing. Paul glanced down and there on

a shelf under the counter was a revolver. He snatched it up, stuck the muzzle in the old man's startled face and said in the toughest voice he could manage, "Let go my arm or I'll blow your head off."

The old man dropped the phone. He let go of Paul, backed against the wall with both hands outstretched to ward Paul off and mumbled, "Easy, boy, easy. No harm done. No harm."

"That's right," Paul said. He walked backward to the door. There he dropped the gun and fled. He was on the highway in seconds and automatically raced along it. He glanced back after a couple of hundred yards. A police car was swinging in at the motel. The old man ran out and climbed in. They'd be coming down this road in seconds.

Off to the left there was a dark mass of trees about half a mile away. They'd spot him crossing this flat land even at night. To the right, across an open field and about a hundred yards away, was the beach and the sea. The black hulk of an old derelict was pulled up on the sand. He jumped down off the road and headed for it.

That moment a powerful spotlight probed the dark.

Paul dove flat in the ditch beside the road. The light beam passed over him and swept the field. The police car passed going slow, the light sweeping a great arc. In that brief flash Paul saw a concrete culvert that ran under the road a few yards off. The car stopped. The two men got out.

The officer said, "He's not on the road, Frank. And

if we got here as fast as you say we did he couldn't have gone any further than we are now. He must have gone some other direction.''

''I saw him start running up this road I tell you. He went right under the streetlight.''

''Well, some of these kids run like deer. Maybe he headed for that grove of trees off there on the left, or someplace else, or maybe it took you a little longer to call me than you think. In the excitement it's pretty easy to be off five or ten minutes. In that length of time he could find a hole or something to crawl into.''

''I wasn't excited; scared sure. Who wouldn't be. I've been through this before. Remember? I called you immediately. I knew where you were. He's got to be hiding right close here. Skinny as he was he could hide behind a shock of grass. Flash your light along this ditch.''

Paul scrambled to the culvert and eased himself inside. The light beam passed him and came back. ''Nothing,'' the officer said.

''I saw something. That culvert that runs under the road.''

''We'll check it.''

''I'll go to the other end.''

''No need.'' The officer laughed. ''The light shines clear through. Come on, Frank, you're getting jittery.''

''You would, too, if you'd looked into the business end of that gun.''

Paul scrambled out of the culvert and lay flat in the

ditch again. The shaft of light lanced past his face, barely missing him.

"Clean as a hound's tooth," the officer said.

There was the sound of feet climbing the enbankment. Paul eased back into the culvert.

"I don't like this even a little bit," the old man grumbled. "I'm sure that kid's around here and mighty close. I don't want the office broken into again like a few months ago. I've seen plenty of these runaway kids the past ten years and I'm telling you this is one of the toughest. His eyes behind my gun were cold as ice. That kid didn't care a hoot if he killed me or not. I want him caught."

"I don't blame you. But I can't leave the patrol car sitting here while I go ramming around these fields in the dark looking for some stray kid. A really important call could come in and I'd miss it."

"All right, if you'll wait here I'll go back and call the school. They'll bring down a bunch of their own kids to hunt him down. They'll find him, too, believe me. It makes the rest hopping mad when one runs away, because that takes privileges away from all of them. They can get here in about fifteen minutes."

"You mean an hour," the officer said. "They'll have to check to see who's missing."

"They know who's missing. They brought a team down here this afternoon and played a game of ball with the town team. Two of their kids sneaked off. They caught one but the other got away. They hunted for him a couple of hours, then they had to get back to the school for evening check-in. Didn't you know about that?''

"I've been gone all day," the officer said. "I just got back in time to go to work. All right, call the school. I'll wait until they come."

Paul lay quiet inside the culvert. He peeked out once. The police car with its flashing light was less than fifty feet away.

Finally a car drew up and he heard voices. "All right, there's twelve of us. We'll split up in parties of three like before. My guess is he's in that stand of timber. That's where we found the other one. You've all got flashlights. Whoever sees him sing out and we'll all move in. If we don't find him we'll meet on the other side of the trees and decide what to do. Let's go."

Paul eased out and raised his head. Dark figures were fanning out across the field. Flashlight beams probed the night. A station wagon was parked nearby. The police car was turning around to return to town. They'd be back. He had to get out of here right now.

He waited until the police car was gone; then crouching low he raced toward the beach and the old boat hulk.

4

The boat lay half on its side. Paul crawled over the broken rail and felt his way into the cabin. There was the smell of mold and dampness and rotting wood. He crouched below a broken window and stared toward the dark ribbon of road.

He hadn't been there long when three boys materialized out of the night, heading for the old derelict. Paul slipped over the far side, took two steps and fell down an almost sheer bank about five feet high. He was on the beach, with the ocean but a few feet away. He ran crouching along the bank, then discovered it abruptly ended. One more step and he'd be out in the open. They'd certainly search along this bank. He couldn't stay here. He raced back, heading for the little dock where the boat was moored. He'd hide in the dark under the dock until the boys left.

The dock's sides were enclosed with heavy planks

nailed about four inches apart. He climbed the side of the dock, using the openings for toe- and hand-holds, and peeked over the top. A second group of boys was closing in. He hung there watching them. There was no place left to go. Then he remembered the boat bumping gently against the face of the dock.

Paul edged swiftly around the dock and dropped silently to the deck. He eased the cabin door open, went inside, and almost fell through an open trapdoor that led down to the pitch-black engine room. He scrambled down a ladder and hid behind the engine.

Through the open port he heard the boys talking as they walked around on the dock. "Well," a voice said, "he ain't around here. If you ask me he's gone on down the highway or maybe somebody in a car picked him up."

"I'd like to have seen old Born's face when Tim shoved his own cannon under his nose."

"Yeah. I'll bet it scared him out of a year's growth."

"I'll bet."

"What about the boat?" someone asked. "We'd better check that out."

"Oh, no, that's old man McKinzie's. Tim wouldn't mess around with him. Let's get out of here."

Paul gave the boys plenty of time to return to the highway and their car before he came out from behind the motor. He was about to climb the ladder when he heard footsteps on the dock and voices again. Men's voices. He peeked out the open port.

Three men were crossing the dock to the boat. Two carried suitcases in each hand. The third carried a bright lantern and swung his right leg in a stiff arc that made him limp badly. A long leather case was slung over his shoulder by a strap. From the shape of it Paul knew it contained a rifle.

A moment later feet crossed the deck and entered the cabin. The trapdoor closed with a bang. Sounds came down clearly from above. A heavy voice that sounded like it was accustomed to giving orders said, "Have you got all my gear on board?"

"Yes, sir, everything's ready to go, Mr. McKinzie. What are you hunting this time?"

"Cougar. A real bruiser if I can believe Frost. More than eight feet in length. Frost says he'll go better than two hundred fifty pounds. I think Frost's stretching the weight a little. You know how he is. But even so it's a big cat."

"I remember. That's the cat I took out there ten or twelve days ago. He's that tame TV cat that went mad and attacked the actor and clawed him up bad. He'll go two fifty easy. He's a mighty big cougar. I thought you'd already killed him."

"No. I wanted to be sure he was wild and ugly, not tame like he used to be. So Frost worked on him. Apparently it took longer than he figured. He just called me last night and said he had him ready."

"How many animals have you killed out there so far?"

"The cougar'll make twenty. Okay, we all set? Then let's get under way."

The starter cut in. The motor began to turn over. The starter ground and ground.

A voice finally said, "I thought you changed those plugs and points."

"I haven't had time. I've been busy. You know that."

"All right. But those old plugs and points are still in there. They should have been changed a week ago."

"I can do it now. It'll only take a few minutes."

"Let it go," McKinzie's voice said. "It's getting late and it looks like we've got a blow coming. If you can get her running let's move out. You can change the plugs and points when we reach the island."

The starter continued to grind. Finally the motor sputtered raggedly to life. It ran unevenly for several minutes, then settled down to a smooth rumble. The boat moved away from the dock. The curl of water at the bow made a soft, creamy sound. They were heading out to sea.

The talk and moving around overhead stopped. Only occasionally did Paul hear a voice. Through the small, open port, the black sea slipped steadily astern. A round chunk of night and stars were visible, but a ceiling of black clouds was slowly blotting them out.

So they were headed for some island. Paul wondered how far it was and how big. There must be people on it since McKinzie was going there. Maybe there was a small town of some kind.

His problem was how to return to the mainland without being caught—that is, if the boat returned. Anyway, when the boat reached the island one of the men was coming down here to work on the motor. That meant he'd be seen and caught unless he found a place to hide.

Paul felt his way about the dim interior. It was small, completely bare except for the motor. There was not a single nook or cranny to hide in. He was trapped like a mouse in a cage.

"They haven't got you yet," he told himself sternly. "You got this far without being detected and you've had some close shaves. Don't give up now. Make them catch you. Keep your wits about you and be ready to take advantage of any kind of break."

He began to reason and plan.

The man who came down wouldn't expect to find anyone. So he would be startled. Maybe for a couple of seconds he'd be frozen into immobility and would neither think nor act. He had to make the most of those seconds. With luck he might duck past the man and get up the ladder into the cabin. The two other men might or might not be in the cabin. If they were he had a good chance of getting away from McKinzie. The stiff leg would make him slow and awkard. As for the other man, once again he'd simply have to take his chances and try. But if he did manage to get away from them he'd have to jump ashore on the island. That prospect didn't appeal to him, but it was preferable to being taken back like some unruly child who had been caught.

He hadn't the faintest idea where he'd go, what he'd

do, or what he'd find on the island. He'd meet those problems if and when he got ashore. As a plan it wasn't much. To be successful, it depended almost entirely on luck and surprise. But it was the only thing he could think of.

His mind was made up, Paul stood beside the open port and watched the ink-black sea flow astern. The storm cloud had blotted out the stars.

For more than an hour the boat rolled and pitched as it bored steadily through the rough seas. Finally the motor slowed. Through the rain-streaked port Paul made out the shape of an island and, close at hand, the black outline of a small dock. The motor was slammed into reverse and raced. A moment later they stopped with a gentle bump. The motor was shut off.

The trapdoor opened. Legs started down the ladder. A voice said, "Where you going?"

"To change those plugs and points."

"Let them go for now. We'll help Mr. McKinzie up to the lodge with his gear first. It'll only take a few minutes. Then you can come back."

The legs disappeared. The trapdoor dropped.

Paul watched the three men, loaded down with luggage, cross the dock and disappear into the black wall of trees. One of them would return in a few minutes. This was his only chance to get off the boat.

Paul climbed the ladder and pushed up on the trapdoor. It rose easily. The moment he stepped out the cabin door, he was slammed by driving wind and rain.

The storm was worse than he'd thought. He ducked his head and followed the men across the dock and into the swaying trees.

Paul found himself on a dim trail that plunged immediately deeper into the forbidding forest. The night was the darkest he'd ever known. The storm clawed at him. He turned up his collar, zipped the jacket to his chin and drove forward, head and shoulders bent against the push of the storm.

Within minutes he came to a fork in the trail. He stopped, trying to decide which he should take. He thought he glimpsed a swinging light down the left fork and heard a robust shout. He took the opposite trail. It felt clear enough underfoot, but it was barely wide enough for one person. Whipping limbs and brush slapped at him as he passed. He hoped the trail led to a house or settlement where he could spend the night.

The pit-black dark was alive with mysterious sounds. At every turn he was tensed for some unnamed horror waiting to spring upon him. Rain puddled the soggy trail, making his footing slippery. It drummed on nearby leaves. The wind-driven force of it stung his face. High above, wind made a roaring through the tree-tops. From the right came the eternal booming of the surf. All about him were indefinable shapes and odd sounds that set his nerves on edge and lifted his heart into his throat.

He teetered on the edge of panic and knew it. The first time he walked out on a stage and looked over the sea of faces, his voice died in his throat. But that was a fear he understood. He was prepared for it. This was nature's fury unleashed. He did not know what to expect or how to meet it.

Some small animal, that he sensed rather than saw, darted across the trail almost under his feet. There was an explosive snort, a crashing of brush as some big animal charged off. The constant scraping and swaying of limbs and trees was an almost human moaning. A wet branch slapped across his face, stinging and almost blinding him. He tripped and sprawled headlong. A tree or limb broke with a rifle-sharp report. He scrambled up, his courage suddenly gone. He began to run headlong down the dark, slippery trail.

Somehow Paul managed to avoid crashing into rocks, stumps and fallen trees. He was sobbing for breath when he burst out of the forest into a clear little glade. There the trail ended. He stopped, panting, his first rush of panic spent. "Cut it out," he told himself. "It's just a storm. You've been in storms before. Not exactly like this one, but storms."

In the others he had had the protection of a car or bus and there had been people with him. He watched the battle of the elements in comfort. This time he was alone and he was truly in it. A storm at night in a strange forest was a really scary thing.

"There's nothing out here to be afraid of," he told himself. Then he remembered the sound of the big body smashing through the brush. And he thought of the huge cougar running loose who had already attacked a man. He looked about fearfully.

There was no sign of a house. The trail had simply stopped at this empty little glade that was whipped by wind and rain and surrounded by a forest of huge trees and thick, impenetrable brush.

Straight across the glade the black bulk of a massive castlelike pile of stone rose out of the forest floor. Its top was as high as the whipping trees. Even in the dark and rain Paul made out the vague shapes of crevices and overhangs. Somewhere up there he might find a dry spot to get out of the storm. But more important he would get out of this forbidding and mysterious forest and off the ground where the cougar stalked.

It was not a particularly hard climb even in the rain and dark. There were many rock outcroppings for foot- and handholds. He had climbed but a few feet when he saw the jutting shape of a ledge about two-thirds the way up. He aimed for the ledge. When he finally stood on top, he discovered it narrowed down and squeezed back into the rock. It formed a dark cave with a roof so low he had to stoop to enter.

Paul felt his way carefully into the black interior. The walls and floor felt fairly smooth and sloped gently downward into the rock mass. A few feet inside he sat down and put his back against the wall. Rain had run off his cap, inside his collar, and trickled down his neck. One shoulder and half his back were soaked. His pants, beneath the waist-length jacket, were wet. For the first time in his life he was cold and miserable. He wrapped his arms about his chest and pulled up his knees to trap the little heat in his body. He thought he might catch a cold and wouldn't be able to sing. Then he smiled a little. Out here, who cared?

Rain ran steadily from the overhang. Beyond he could just make out the tops of the trees being tortured by the wind. The sounds of the storm were muted, bringing an eerie unreality to the night he'd not felt before. Now that he had time to think, there was something very strange about this island, and about at least one of the people who'd come out here.

This man, McKinzie, who came to kill one special animal that had been brought here for that purpose. A cougar, once tame, that had been provoked until it was wild and dangerous again just to give McKinzie more pleasure in the hunt. He had killed nineteen other animals that Paul guessed had been transported here for his pleasure. Apparently McKinzie loved to kill. Trails that led nowhere. A man whose job it was to make tame animals mean. What sort of island was this and what kind of men were these? Paul began to suspect there'd be no town, maybe no homes, only the lodge. What had he let himself in for?

Huddled there shivering and hungry, a storm raging a few feet away, Paul began to feel small and helpless, a child hanging on the edge of terror.

For the first time he saw this escape as an ill-conceived, poorly planned and badly timed stunt that was backfiring on him. This had to be the end. He'd gone as far as he could. There was nothing left to do but face the humiliation of being taken back. He'd have to find some other way to convince his parents and Mr. Matthews.

He could return to the boat and tell them who he was. They'd take him back to the mainland. But the thought of stumbling back down that dark trail in this storm, with a vicious cougar on the loose, was more than he could face. Besides, the boat had probably left by now. He'd wait until morning, then hunt up that lodge and tell them who he was. With that decided he settled back to wait out the long night hours.

He was dozing off when a piercing scream stabbed the night like a driven knife. It jerked him wide awake. The scream came again, like a human voice in agony. For a moment the very force of it seemed to still the storm. High-pitched and eerie it rode the wind, coming from everywhere and nowhere. It was a part of this wild and mysterious night and this strange island and its forbidding forest and strange people.

Fear gushed through Paul. He surged to hands and knees and began groping frantically for some kind of weapon. His hand found a baseball-sized rock and gripped it. The scream did not come again. With just the sounds of the wind and rain and the creaking and groaning of trees, the night was strangely quiet.

Paul crouched on his knees a long time, gripping the rock, ears straining to catalog every sound. His eyes stared into the night for the least movement of some vague, menacing shape. But no fierce monster charged through the cave's black opening to bear down upon him. Finally he sank back against the wall, the rock gripped, ready in his hand. All thought of sleep was gone. He meant to stay awake the rest of the night.

The first gray light of dawn faded into the cave. Paul rubbed his eyes and pulled himself into a more upright position. He didn't know what had roused him, but he still had a vague sense of dread.

The rain had stopped. There was no sound of groaning, creaking trees. The storm had passed. His pants were still wet. His legs felt numb with cold. Sometime during the night he had dropped the rock and it had rolled down the slope. He looked about the dim interior. The cave ran back about ten feet, the floor sloped downward. It was surprisingly clear of litter. The ceiling was high enough to stand erect.

Then his eyes went to the opening and he froze. For one moment his heart seemed to stop. Then it began to race. Standing in the cave entrance, outlined against the pale dawn, was the black shape of an enormous cat. Its stubby ears were pricked forward. Its yellow eyes shone like live coals in the first light. Its lips lifted in a silent snarl, exposing long tearing teeth. Then its eyes narrowed and the end of the long tail snapped from side to side. Paul sensed its whole sinewy body drawing tightly together as if to spring.

The cat stood statue-still, studying him for what seemed an eternity. Its gaze was as direct and probing as any Paul had ever encountered. Then it moved into the cave. Its big soft paws made not a whisper of sound. Frozen with fear he watched it come straight toward him.

5

Paul was too terrified to breathe. He thought fleetingly of the rock he'd dropped while he slept. He was afraid to shift his eyes for even a second to look for it. But it would do no good against this animal. It might even make him more vicious. This had to be the cat brought out here for McKinley to hunt. The cat that had gone mad and already attacked one man; that another man had spent days deliberately making mean and ugly.

Paul pressed his back tight against the wall and watched in horrified fascination as the cat padded deliberately, soundlessly toward him. He was aware of the heavy scent of the animal's wet fur. He was completely at the animal's mercy. He wanted to scream but his throat was paralyzed.

He shut his eyes, tensed his body and waited—waited for the cat's great weight to crash into him, the gleaming teeth to plunge into him, the rip of powerful claws in his flesh.

The cat was upon him. He heard the soft rasp of its breath. Then a warm, rough tongue licked his cheek. It happened a second time before he opened his eyes fearfully. The cat's face was not a foot away. Again the wet tongue came out and licked his face. There was a soft rumble in the animal's throat. It had begun to purr.

Paul drew a sobbing, careful breath and tried to speak. It was the second time before any sound came. Then it was no more than a husky whisper. "You're not mad are you. You're not mad at all. I sure am glad!"

The cat lay down close against him, began to lick a wet paw and continued to purr.

Finally Paul raised a hand and very lightly, carefully, touched the cat's head between the stubby ears. The head came up immediately against his hand, and automatically he scratched lightly at the wet fur. The cat closed his eyes and purred louder. He rolled his head so that Paul scratched first one ear, then the other. Experimentally he increased the pressure and scratched harder. The cat loved it. He brought up the other hand and scratched both ears at the same time. The cat raised its head higher in sheer ecstasy, rubbed its head against Paul's chest, then licked Paul's chin.

Fear left Paul. He continued to scratch and said softly, "Why, you're not vicious at all. You're all right. I think you're great! What'd that man do that made you attack him? I'll bet he teased you or was mean. I don't blame you. You had a right to fight back." The cat kept rubbing his head against Paul and purring as if he had been lonesome and had found a friend.

The cat stretched his long, sleek length out against Paul, yawned hugely, dropped his head on his paws and closed his eyes. Paul didn't want to move to disturb him, and the warmth of the cat's body felt good against his cold legs. He couldn't resist the temptation to take this warmth. Carefully, slowly, he slid down, stretching his own body beside that of the cat. He let his body go slack against the other's warm softness. The last thing he remembered was the contented purring a few inches from his face.

When Paul awoke the sun was streaming into the cave entrance. He guessed it must be about nine o'clock. Sometime while he slept he laid his arm across the cat's shoulders and snuggled his body closer for warmth. Now his face was pressed almost in the fur of the cat's neck. He lay there for some minutes basking in the warmth and comfort of the great cat's body. He kept telling himself what an amazing experience this was. Yet it seemed so completely natural. Carefully he raised himself on an elbow and looked down at the sleeping cat. He lay stretched full length on his side. One big paw was over his eyes to shut out the sun. His coat was now dry and glistened. Paul couldn't resist the temptation to lightly stroke the silken shoulder.

Paul had never had any kind of pet. It might scratch or bite, or carry some kind of disease that could lead to his being ill and the cancellation of an appearance. The cat made a gurgling sound at his touch but he did not open his eyes. The black tip of his tail thumped the floor in recognition of the stroking hand. Paul smiled, thinking if only his parents and Mr. Matthews could see him now. His mother would probably go into hysterics.

He remembered that this morning he was going to hunt up the lodge and let the people there take him back to Seattle. He hated to leave the cat behind, especially since that limping man, McKinzie, had come out here to try to kill it. But, he reasoned, the cat was big and powerful and very sly. The man was something of a cripple. His movements were slow and jerky. The island seemed to be covered with a forest. There must be plenty of places to hide. And look at the cat. He wasn't worried. Whether wild or tame, all animals knew how to take care of themselves. It was too bad, but the cat would have to look out for himself even as he was doing. "The fact is you're better equipped to take care of yourself than I am," he told the cat in a low voice, "and I'm doing it."

Paul moved carefully away from the cat, stood up and went to the entrance and looked out. The morning was rain-washed and diamond-clear. The sun had not yet broken above the treetops and the forest was lanced with golden light shafts. Not a leaf stirred. The silence was complete.

The ledge was a little more than halfway up the rock pile, and the climb from the little glade below was not bad for about the first forty feet. The last twenty or so the climber had to pick his way from rock to rock. Paul wondered idly why he hadn't slipped and fallen last night.

He looked back at the cat sleeping peacefully in the

inner cave and said under his breath, "Good-bye, cat. Thanks for keeping me warm this morning. Good luck. I hope you can keep away from McKinzie." Then he turned to go. He felt an odd sense of loss and sadness at leaving the cat here alone.

Two men stepped into the little glade below. Paul dropped to hands and knees and slid back so he'd not be seen. There was a foot-deep crevice in the lip of the ledge, and looking through this he could watch the men in the glade without being seen. They seemed to be looking right at the cave entrance. The one in the black-and-red plaid jacket was Mr. McKinzie of the stiff leg. Now he carried a powerful-looking rifle in the crook of his arm. The other man was tall and thin. He carried no rifle. Paul could hear them plainly.

The thin man was saying, "I only came along this morning, Mr. McKinzie, to show you the places I've seen the cat most often. This is not one of them."

McKinzie said in the heavy, authoritative voice Paul remembered, "That pile of rock with the cave up there is a mighty good place for a cat to lay up. They like high places where they can look around and caves to sleep in."

"That's normally correct," the thin man said, "but in the ten days I chased this cat around the island I never once found him up there."

"You climbed up and looked in the cave?"

"No, sir, it didn't seem necessary. I've found that cat just about everyplace else on the island but there. But I'll go up now if you want me to."

"If he's in there you'd scare him out sure. You'd be right in line so I couldn't shoot. I'll go up. He's my cat."

"Climbing up there could be dangerous. You might slip and fall."

"You don't think I can make it?"

"I didn't say that. But it rained hard last night. Every spot the sun hasn't hit is slick. Why take the chance when there's an easier way."

"What is it?"

"Put a couple of shots into that cave. I guarantee that if he's in there he'll come charging out like a scalded cat. I've got that cougar so gun-shy he about throws a fit every time he hears a gun go off."

"That's what you did?"

"A couple of times. Nothing happened. I don't think he likes that particular cave. It's too big, too roomy for a cat to feel comfortable. But try it."

"All right." McKinzie raised the rifle. To Paul it seemed the muzzle was pointed right at his head. Frantically he shoved himself backward down the incline of the cave floor and waited.

The sound of the shot was enormous. It shattered the morning and lunged into the cave in deafening waves. It filled all space and smashed against the walls and eardrums with hammer force. In the ceiling at the back of the cave a rock exploded into dust where the heavy slug hit. Then, as quickly, there was silence.

The cat was on his feet, crouched, yellow eyes wild with fright. He was about to bolt out the entrance.

"No!" Paul whispered. "Oh, no! You'll be killed!" Without thinking he slid down to the cat, put both arms around its neck and pressed it back to the floor. "Be quiet," he whispered. "It's all right. It's all right. He can't see you. Stay! Stay!" Whether it was the sound of his voice, his stroking hands, or the cat had been so well trained that it automatically reacted to human commands even when terrified, he didn't know. But it lay crouched on the floor, tense and trembling under his hands. He could feel the trip-hammer beat of its heart.

Again the rifle tore the silence apart. The thunderclap of sound rolled up and into the cave. In the ceiling a chunk of rock burst and showered them with fragments. The cat jumped and made a small moaning sound of fright.

Paul held it tighter. His hands caressed it and he spoke softly, reassuringly. "It's all right. Don't move. Don't move. I won't let anything happen to you. Lie still. Be quiet."

The cat continued to moan and tremble, but it did not try to jump and run.

A third shot followed. This time it was all Paul could do to hold the cat from bolting out the cave. He waited for a fourth shot, fearful that he could no longer hold the cat. It did not come, and finally he said softly, "It's all right now. It's all over. That's all. There's nothing to be afraid of now."

Paul kept petting and talking to the cat in a low, intimate voice. Finally he stopped trembling, his heartbeat slowed and he began to purr. He rolled onto his back, all four feet in the air, and invited Paul to scratch his stomach. Paul did, smiling. "You're not afraid anymore," he said. "That's good. I wish I could forget some things that easy." The cat rolled back on his side, put a paw over his eyes to shut out the light and contentedly went to sleep.

Paul rose and stood looking down at the cat. He'd never dreamed such a big, fearsome animal could be so frightened. It knew what the sound of the gun meant. Somehow it seemed to be aware that the man was trying to kill it, or at least it recognized deadly danger in the sound of the rifle.

Paul thought of the cougar. The cat wanted to live as much as he did. It had once been tame and trusted people. Then it was brought out here into a strange land, tormented until ugly and frightened, and then hunted. Now it was confused and deathly afraid. It could only react in two ways, fight or run. It wanted to run. Paul could still feel the cat's body trembling under his hands. The moaning sounds of its terror. In its fear the cat had put complete trust in him and had remained still. Never before had he been called upon to protect or care for any living thing. That changed everything. He felt big and strong and fiercely protective.

Now it was terribly important to him that the cat live. In comparison to the cat's, his own problem sank into insignificance. He could not leave this island and let the cat face the hunter alone. He had to stay and do everything possible to protect him.

Paul returned to the cave entrance. The sun was well

above the treetops and was pouring its heat onto the earth. The little glade was empty. He was ravenously hungry and thirsty. He guessed the cat would sleep a few hours. That would give him time to look for something to eat and drink.

Paul picked his way carefully down the rock pile, crossed the little glade and entered the timber. The sun was warming the soggy earth. The thin mustiness of steam rose to meet him. He came into a trail and followed it. He hadn't progressed far when a rabbit hopped across the trail, stopped beside a log in plain sight and began to feed on the leaves of a low plant. Rabbits were good eating. If he could kill one he'd manage to cook it somehow. He bent slowly, keeping his eyes on the rabbit, found a rock and rose. He drew back his arm carefully, then suddenly fired the rock with all his strength. He missed by a foot. The rabbit made two startled leaps and disappeared.

Paul filled his pockets with rocks and went on. Squirrels and chipmunks scampered about on limbs and chattered at him. Birds flitted through the trees, scolding and chirping. He frightened up a grouse and a pheasant. Crows kept talking. He hadn't realized a forest could be so noisy. He saw another rabbit and tried again with a rock, and missed. He kept seeing rabbits and throwing until he was out of rocks. He crossed and recrossed trails. Several times the one he was following branched. Paul carefully noted each branch so he could return.

Finally, a trail he was following skirted a meadow and ran beside a blackberry patch. Ripe berries hung to the vines in clusters. Paul tasted them. They were good. He began cramming his mouth as fast as he could pick them. They satisfied his hunger and the juice temporarily quenched his thirst. He moved about the patch, eating until he was full.

He had been gone some time. The sun was almost overhead and the heat soaked through his jacket. The cat would probably be waking soon. He'd better return to the cave. He didn't want him prowling the woods while McKinzie was abroad looking for him.

Paul began retracing his steps carefully. While the blackberries had helped quench his thirst, he was still thirsty. He kept passing pools of water. Some were full of swimming bugs. Others were half covered with green slime. A sluggish, slow-moving stream was not clear and he didn't like the plants that were growing in the water. None of the water he passed seemed drinkable.

He came to the edge of the little glade and was about to step into it when he saw McKinzie standing there looking up at the cave. Luckily his feet had made no sound on the soft trail.

Paul stepped quickly behind a tree. He had his first close look at the man who'd come to kill the tame cougar. He was big. He'd shed his plaid jacket, tied the sleeves around his waist and let it hang down the backs of his legs. He was broad shouldered, thick chested. He had a shock of black hair, scowling black brows and a belligerent chin. His pale skin, beaded with sweat on this hot day, looked cold. He turned his head slightly and his eyes were blue, deep-set and without warmth.

Paul knew he was looking at a man who did not hunt for sport, but for the sheer love of killing. He looked like a man who could kill nineteen animals that had been imported here for him and enjoy every second of it. The thought was like a cold breeze chilling him.

McKinzie looked up at the cave entrance and fiddled with the bolt of the rifle. Paul knew he was debating shooting into the cave again. He held his breath. McKinzie's heavy face was scowling, intent. Finally he dropped the rifle to the crook of his arm, swung stiffly across the glade and disappeared.

6

Paul ran to the rock pile, climbed swiftly to the cave and entered. The cat was gone. He returned outside and stood on the ledge and looked about. Beneath, the forest floor lay bright and warm and still. Not a branch or a leaf moved. The odors of the island drifted up to him, a mixture of wildness, of growth and ancient decay that seemed stronger up here than when he walked the forest floor.

The cat could be anywhere. Paul hoped he wouldn't run into McKinzie. From where he stood the tops of the tallest trees were several feet above him. The crown of the rock pile was as high as the trees. It appeared to end in a flat, tablelike square. The cat could be lying up there sunning himself. The climb looked reasonably easy. He started up.

The top was about a ten-foot square slab of almost flat rock. From it he looked out over the tops of the trees. He could see the white line of the distant surf and the sea. Nowhere was there a settlement or even a house. The island looked completely wild except for the trails he could see threading their way through the timber. It was warm and pleasant up here. The blackberries had temporarily satisfied his hunger and at the moment his thirst was not bothering him.

He stretched out flat on the rock and stared up at the sky. He found himself thinking of the gang of boys he'd played ball with in the vacant lot. Was it just two days ago? It seemed ages; so much had happened. He smiled to himself. This was certainly like Bud's lying on his back on the Skyline Trail watching the clouds sail past. And it was a lot more exciting and daring than sleeping on the trail. None of that gang had slept with a cougar inside a cave and been shot at with a high-powered rifle. He'd not only caught up with their exciting experiences, he'd passed them.

He wondered idly what his parents and manager, Henry Matthews, were doing—and the police. Don't forget the whole state full of police were looking for him. Then he thought about the concert he'd missed, the songs that had been planned for that night.

Several would have been new, others from recent albums. They had planned to close the show with "Wintertime." He lay listening to a soft breeze begin whispering through the near trees, the distant sound of the surf, the far-off voices of gulls. There was a kind of music in the very air here.

He had recorded one number recently with lyrics that, amazingly, just fit the situation he was in now. It had been written especially for him. It was a soft, sad song about a boy going home after a long absence. He began to hum. The lyrics were perfect:

> The sky has turned to a purple haze.
> I gotta leave. I just can't stay.
> I'm going.
> I was born so far away,
> Seems so near, just yesterday.
> I'm going.
>
> Clouds in the sky touch my face.
> I'll go find another place.
> I'm going.
> Clouds in the sky touch the ground,
> I'll go find another sound.
> I'm going.
>
> Stars look down and I'm alone.
> My head's spinning round,
> I'm going home.
> I'm leaving on the evening train,
> I'll be gone before it starts to rain.
> I'm going.
>
> Rustling leaves that slow my feet,
> Running down an empty street.
> I'm g-o-i-n-g.

He felt he could do much better now. The lyrics meant something to him. When he returned he'd see that the next concert closed with "I'm Going."

Paul sat up and thought about himself, where he was, and what he was going to do. He couldn't live indefinitely on blackberries, and he was getting thirsty again. What would be the end of this?

It was impossible to work out a plan of action. He didn't know where to begin. From here on everything had to be taken one step at a time, played by ear so to speak, just like some concerts. He'd sing a slow number and the audience would sit on their hands. He'd come back with a fast one and they'd almost tear the roof off. He had to be ready to change here, too, take advantage of whatever opportunity presented itself.

He didn't hear a sound, but suddenly the cougar was beside him. Paul patted his small head, scratched at the base of his ears and under his chin. The cat lay down beside him, completely relaxed, stretched out his neck and began to purr. Paul said, "Mr. McKinzie was here looking for you. Quit chasing around in the daylight. You could run into him and that would be the last of you." The cat licked a front paw, rubbed it across his face, then turned on his side and closed his eyes.

Paul didn't know how long they lay there side by side, warmed by the sun and the rock beneath them. Paul dozed and so did the cougar. The sun had swung three-quarters down the sky and was again behind the treetops when the cat raised his head. His ears shot forward. His yellow eyes narrowed and his whole body became tense.

Paul raised himself slightly and looked down in the direction the cat faced. There was McKinzie swinging stiffly across the little glade again. He pressed the cat's head down and dropped his own. "Be still," he whispered. "Don't move. Don't move."

Paul waited several minutes. When he eased his head up again the glade was empty. McKinzie was a dogged, persistent hunter.

The first shadows of evening moved across the glade and up the rocks. A cool breeze came in from the sea. The cougar rose, stretched and started leisurely down off the rock pinnacle. Paul followed, hoping McKinzie had called off his hunt for the day.

He was hungry again.

They crossed the glade and came into the trail. Here under the thick canopy of trees it was almost night. The cat was a tawny shadow padding silently a step ahead, as if he'd been trained to walk there. The cat seemed to know where he was going, so Paul followed. Paul was trying to keep a sharp lookout for McKinzie in the gathering dusk and almost ran into the cat. He had stopped. He turned his head right and left. The white butterfly patch under his nose twitched as he cast for some scent. Then his long body crouched. The stubby ears came forward. The small head was stretched out straight. He began to move through the gloom like a wraith.

A small fear pulsed through Paul. Here was the hunter incarnate. His every look and action personified all that was fierce and deadly. Paul let the cat get a dozen steps ahead; then he followed as silently as possible. At a turn in the trail the cat crouched belly-flat to the ground. He seemed to flow forward, taking advantage of every rock, bush and shadow. So great was its concentration, Paul knew that for the moment he did not exist. Every muscle, nerve and faculty was centered on the stalk, the kill. One moment the animal was rock-still; the next he was catapulting silently through the night, powerful forelegs outstretched. There was a single squeak of surprise and fright. Then silence.

Paul walked around the bend. The cat crouched in the trail tearing open a rabbit. He sat on a rock and waited while the cat relished his meal. Again he was the gentle, purring cat who rubbed against him and licked his face. Watching the cat made the saliva run in Paul's mouth.

The cat disposed of the rabbit in a few minutes, then set off along the trail again. Paul followed. Finally the cat turned off the trail. He led Paul through the brush to a small, clear spring that bubbled up between two big rocks. The cat drank, then sat down, daintily shook each paw and began washing his face with his wrist.

Paul stretched out on the ground beside the cat and drank his fill. The water was sweet and cold. It made his teeth ache. When he finished he said, "How did you find this spring? I walked right past it. I guess there are a lot of things you know that I don't. Now, maybe you can find me something to eat. I'm half-starved."

The cat leisurely finished washing, then rose and returned to the trail. Once again Paul followed a step behind. The sun was completely gone. Here under the canopy of giant trees, night was a thick cloak thrown loosely over the land. The trail was a darker thread that wandered aimlessly through the night. The breeze turned cooler. Paul zipped up his facket against its chill.

Finally the cat turned into a narrower side trail. The only sounds were those of Paul's clothing scraping against an occasional bush or limb. They emerged from the trees and before them was a large log building with several smaller outbuildings. Paul studied the larger one. This must be the lodge. Its walls were of logs. It was two-storied and had a long, wide porch running across the front. Through a front window he saw lights burning somewhere in back. There was no other sign anyone was here.

The cat walked purposefully around a corner of the lodge. Paul followed, ready to duck at the first sign of life. The cat went straight to a small building and padded around it to a door. He sniffed along the crack at the bottom of the door, then reared up and pawed at the hasp until it rattled. Paul shoved him aside. "Cut that out," he whispered. "You want somebody to come out and catch us?"

The hasp had a bolt dropped through a ring to hold the door closed. The cat had apparently smelled something. Paul put his nose to the crack and he caught the faint aroma. He removed the bolt and cautiously opened the door. His nostrils were immediately assailed by mouth-watering odors.

The cat crowded past him and walked inside. Paul followed and closed the door. It was dead-black. He felt along the wall, found a switch and snapped on the light. There were no windows. He figured they were safe from detection.

80

The building was a food storehouse. The walls were lined with shelves loaded with canned goods. There were also loaves of bread, packaged dry foods, flour, sugar, even vegetables and fresh fruit. A huge freezer stood in one corner. There were pots and pans and rows of knives hanging along one wall. Haunches of dried meat hung from the ceiling. The cat sniffed about among the shelves and toppled several cans to the floor. Paul replaced them and whispered, "Cut it out. You want us to get caught?"

There were whole stacks of canned sardines. Paul put two in his pocket. He rearranged the rest so they wouldn't be missed. He took a load of bread and shoved the remaining loaves together. One shelf was full of one-pound cans of ham. He took two, then added another for the cat. He took down about a five-pound piece of dried meat from the ceiling. He needed something to open cans and put the smallest knife on the wall into his pocket. Carrying his precious food he snapped off the light, opened the door and peeked out. The light still shone at the back of the lodge, but all was quiet. The cat and he stole off through the dark trees.

Once again the cat led the way as if he'd been over this ground many times. In a clear spot where the moon shone through the tree foliage, Paul sat on a rock. The cat sat on his tail and looked up expectantly.

"We eat," Paul said, "I'm about starved." He carefully hacked open two of the cans of ham. One he emptied on the ground for the cat. The cat smelled tentatively, then licked the strange food. Finally he settled down and began to eat. Paul tore open the loaf of bread, cut slices from his can of ham, and began cramming it into his mouth. "It may not be as good as fresh rabbit to you," he said to the cat, "but it's a lot better to me."

Paul wolfed the whole can of ham and almost a third of the loaf of bread. Then he sliced chunks of meat from the dried chunk. The cat had finished his ham and watched him expectantly. "You could catch another rabbit," Paul suggested. But he offered the cat a piece. He took it daintily. Thereafter Paul gave the cat every other slice.

Finally he said, "That's enough. I'm full and you ought to be." He smashed the two empty cans flat and buried them in the soft earth. He didn't want anyone to find them and jump to the conclusion someone had broken into the storehouse.

The cat padded down the trail again, a silent reassuring shadow always a step ahead. Paul followed carrying the remainder of the food. Last night during the storm he'd been terrified at the thought this animal might attack him. Now he walked a strange trail in the black of night with the animal, and its presence made him feel perfectly safe. "I sure am glad you're along," he told the cat. The cat turned his head as if listening but didn't slacken his pace.

Paul wanted to return to the cave. But in the dark he was lost. He had no choice but to stay close to the cat and hope he would eventually head back to the cave or they'd come to some spot Paul recognized. They crossed trails, skirted moonlit glades and walked beside dank-smelling ponds and dark brush patches. Rabbits thumped away. An owl ghosted low over their heads and faded into the trees. In the distance a pair of night birds intermittently broke the silence with eerie cries.

They quit the trees and were on the beach. The cat paced along the water's edge for some distance. Then, where a point of land jutted into the sea, he waded belly-deep and stood there as if trying to see beyond the water and the night.

Paul asked softly, "Are you looking for a way to go home? I know how you feel. But you'd better forget it. You could never swim to the mainland. I know. It took us over an hour to cross that water by boat last night. And we traveled a lot faster than you can swim. You're stuck here, at least for now, and it looks like I am, too."

The cat looked at him over his shoulder, listening as if he understood. Then he waded ashore, rubbed his wet side against Paul's legs and began to purr. Paul patted his head. "Just take it easy. You and I are going to work this out together. Somehow we'll beat that old McKinzie."

The cougar started off again, pacing up the beach, keeping close to the water's edge. He turned his head often and looked, but he did not again wade into the sea.

They ran out of beach when the brush grew right down into the water. The cat climbed the bank and turned into a well-defined trail. He seemed completely unconcerned, but Paul could see the stubby ears move, the long tail curl lazily, the head swing from side to side as his amber eyes saw things Paul was not aware of. He was cataloging every wayward scent and night movement.

Eventually they came out near the little dock and Paul knew where he was. He guessed they must have circled almost half the island. His legs were tired. Paul stopped and the cat looked at him. "You go ahead," Paul said, "you're a night animal. It's your nature to prowl. It's not mine. I'm not going to wander over the rest of this island with you. I'm tired. I'm going back to the cave and get some sleep. I wish you'd come with me, but I know you won't." Paul patted the cat between the ears.

The cat's long tail curled right, then left. He lifted his head high and closed his eyes to receive the pat.

"I'll see you in the morning. Just be careful and get back early. Don't let that McKinzie see you."

Paul left the cat standing there looking after him and took the trail to the rock pile.

At the cave Paul felt around in the dark, found a little ledge and put the food upon it. He made himself as comfortable as possible with his back against the cave wall and was prepared to sleep.

Tired as he was sleep would not come. It was a little like after a concert. He was tired, but too keyed up to rest. He kept thinking of the cat and this day, and he also thought of his parents and the time he'd been away. It was three days now. He felt he'd proved he could take care of himself. He was sure they'd see it that way, too, and treat him differently. But he couldn't leave the cat here to be hunted down and killed by this cold-eyed McKinzie.

It was strange how everything seemed to be tied in together—his returning home, what he was trying to prove and saving the cat's life. Saving the cat was the key to the rest. Maybe he could somehow stop a fishing boat and get them to take the cat off the island. But he hadn't seen many boats. Maybe the cat and he could go on dodging McKinzie until he got tired of hunting and quit. But that wasn't likely. He was still trying to think of some way to save the cat when he fell asleep.

7

The sun was lighting the interior of the cave when Paul awoke. The cougar had returned and lay stretched out beside him asleep. One big paw was over its eyes to shut out the morning light. Paul raised himself on an elbow and studied the cat, smiling. He put out a hand and patted the silky-soft shoulder. The cat made a gurgling sound in his throat. The black tip of his tail tapped the floor, but he did not open his eyes. "You go rambling around the country all night," Paul said, "then you want to sleep all day. I could use some company." The black tip tapped the floor again.

Paul eased himself away from the cat and rose. He was hungry and went to the shelf where he'd left the food. He got two slices of bread, hacked open one of the cans of sardines and made himself a sandwich. There were five slices left, two and a half sandwiches. He'd finish the loaf today. That meant another trip to the food cache at the lodge for more. He couldn't do that too often. Somebody would surely miss the food and become suspicious. Then both he and the cat would be in trouble. This couldn't go on much longer without detection.

He stood in the cave entrance eating, watching the sun stab bright lances through the trees, and thinking. Mornings were best for thinking and planning. He always went over the previous night's performance in the morning. Then his mind was clear, uncluttered by unimportant things. He'd made a couple of good suggestions in the past, but no one paid any attention. It would be different when he went back.

With luck he could get away with maybe two more trips to the food cache without their missing anything— if he didn't take too much. If he was careful he could stretch that food to about four days' eating. Then something would have to happen. But what?

He could always walk into the lodge and tell them who he was. He'd be all right. But what about the cat?

He couldn't leave the cat here alone. Then he was struck with another disturbing thought. The cat had returned to sleep early yesterday morning. When he returned from the blackberry patch about noon the cat was gone again. It had shown up later in the afternoon. Apparently that was its pattern. Nap in the morning, ramble around in the afternoon, nap again before taking off for the night. To protect the cat he had to keep it here in the cave, especially during the daylight hours. But how could he do that?

A half-dozen gulls drifted over, letting the air currents

ferry them toward the distant beach. A pair of jays scolded in the brush below. They had no problems. The solution was there and it was so simple and logical he was surprised he hadn't thought of it before. He could settle the problem of himself and the cat in a few minutes, this very morning.

If it was like yesterday the cat would sleep for several more hours. He guessed by the sun it was still more than an hour earlier than McKenzie's visit yesterday morning. If he hurried he could catch the hunter before he left the lodge, make his proposition, and return before the cat awoke.

Paul scrambled down the rock pile and hurried along the trail.

The lodge looked much bigger in daylight. Several wings jutted out in back and there was a long lean-to filled with split wood. No one was in sight. Paul climbed the steps and knocked on the front door.

The man who opened the door was short, barely taller than Paul. He had a big man's chest and shoulders on stubby, bowed legs. His skin was dark, as if from a deep tan. His black eyes were the sharpest Paul had ever seen. He said in a surprisingly soft voice, "Good morning, sonny. You saved me a hike. I was about to start out looking for you."

"For me?" Paul said surprised.

"For you."

"Oh, oh, I see!" But he didn't. "Well, I—I'm Paul Winters."

"All right. I believe you," the Indian smiled. "Now

what do I do, turn handsprings, applaud, or something?''

Paul just stood there. His name or his face always brought some reaction. His thinking was knocked completely off track.

The little man swung the door wide. ''Well, come in, Paul. Come in. We don't get much company out here as you can guess. I'm Joe Ironwood, caretaker and chief cook and bottle washer of this here mansion. So your name's Paul. What can I do for you, Paul?''

Paul had forgotten the speech he'd prepared and asked, ''How did you know about me?''

''I know about you and Sandy, especially about Sandy.''

''Sandy?''

''The cougar. His name's Sandy. You both left tracks all over the place last night. But don't worry. I wiped them out. I've been wiping out Sandy's for days. How come you were with that cat and don't know his name? I wanted to ask you that and other questions this morning. Such as, what are you doing on this island to begin with? How'd you get here? Nobody, but nobody, comes out here except by special invitation from Limpy George McKinzie. I don't figure you had one.''

Paul shook his head. ''I want to talk to the man who's hunting the cougar, Sandy. A big man that limps. I guess that's Mr. McKinzie.''

Joe Ironwood wasn't listening. His sharp black eyes were fixed on Paul with the same look of surprise that had been on the kids' faces the other day when they were playing softball. "Whoa," he said softly. "Back up, sonny. Run that name past me again. Winters, Paul Winters! Sure!" He snapped his fingers. "The boy singer! The hotshot recording and concert star that disappeared suddenly from a motel room in Seattle a few days ago. I heard a broadcast not an hour ago telling how every law officer in the state's on the lookout for you. You've about turned this state upside down. How in the name of all that's holy did you get out here, and how come you and Sandy have teamed up?"

"It's a long story," Paul said. "Right now I want to see this Mr. McKinzie."

"We'll get to him in due time. First you come in here and tell me how come you ran away. That's what you did. Right? How come you got on this island and then tied up with Sandy. You're a real mystery, sonny. And I don't like mysteries." He pulled Paul into the room and closed the door.

Paul sat in a chair in the big beamed living room and asked, "You want to hear it all?"

"Do I want to hear it all?" Ironwood was amazed. "You breeze in here calm as a summer day, a kid that's got the whole state's police force tied in knots, that's front page news in all the papers, on radio, on television. Out of a clear sky you show up here, on this private island, ten miles off the coast—an island where nobody comes without an invitation—and calmly announce you want to see George McKinzie about that cougar he's hunting. On top of that you and the cougar have teamed up. Do I want to hear it all? You can bet

90

your bottom dollar I do. Start at the beginning, sonny. The very beginning. Give me all of it.''

"I guess it does sound a little odd," Paul agreed.

"That's the understatement of the week, sonny. So, start talking."

Paul began with the softball game at the motel. Step by step he told Ironwood everything, right down to McKinzie shooting into the cave and his leaving the cat asleep this morning. He ended by explaining what he hoped to accomplish by his own disappearance.

"Wait a minute," Ironwood said. "You say McKinzie shot into that cave, with you and the cat inside, and he didn't run out?"

"He wanted to. I held him down. It wasn't easy."

Ironwood sat shaking his head. "It's hard to believe. The whole darned story's hard to believe. But nobody, not even a singer-actor like you could make up a story like this. Crazy as it is, how you got here and all, makes a lot of sense. Why you left I can understand a lot better than most people would. I had a problem similar to yours a few months back. I walked away from mine. You left to try to shock your folks into seeing the light. I hope it works. Now, what is it you want to see Limpy McKinzie about?"

"I think I've been gone long enough. I thought he might take me back on the boat."

"No problem there. The launch will be coming back this afternoon with Alec Frost. He went to the mainland for supplies. We can put you on board. We've even got a shortwave here and we can call Seattle and alert your

91

folks and the police that you're on the way home and well."

". . . And I want to save Sandy," Paul finished.

"Save him? You mean keep McKinzie from killing him?"

Ironwood asked surprised. "Not a chance. You don't know what you're getting into there. Anyway, how did you figure to save Sandy?"

"I'll buy him," Paul said promptly. When Ironwood shook his head, Paul added, "I've made plenty of money. I can get it from my parents and my manager."

"You're a minor," Ironwood explained, "how would you get it if they said no, which most any parent would do to buying a full-grown cougar for a son. And from what you've told me, your parents would throw a couple of Grade A fits."

"I'd refuse to sing again until they did," Paul said promptly.

"I'll pay Mr. McKinzie double what he paid for Sandy. That's a good profit."

"Very good," Ironwood agreed. "But old Limpy McKinzie has plenty of money. He has a lot more than you have. His family has been piling it up as big lumbermen for half a century. So money is no inducement, not even if you offered him ten or twenty times what he paid for Sandy. He wants Sandy mounted and in his trophy room so he can tell all his friends exactly how he stalked and killed the biggest cat in North America."

"He likes to kill," Paul said, remembering the expression on McKinzie's face yesterday afternoon as he looked up at the cave.

"Naturally. He's a big game hunter, or he was until he got hurt and could no longer climb or hike very far. Now he has to get his sport by having the game brought onto the island for him where he can hunt it down with little effort and make his kills."

"He calls that sport?"

"A lot of them do."

"You don't like it either," Paul said.

"No more than you do."

"Then help me save Sandy."

"I've thought of it, and not only with Sandy. But I always come smack up aginst one big question. How?"

Paul thought about it; then he said in a careful voice, "We could steal him."

Ironwood nodded. "For the sake of argument let's say we could. What would you do with him? He's a big cat. You couldn't keep him in the city like a dog or house cat. There's a law against keeping wild animals."

"I'd take him out someplace and turn him loose."

"A nice idea. Now we're back to the first part of your problem. To steal him you've got to get off the island. How do you propose to do that?"

"We could sneak him off by boat."

"It would have to be by boat. But only one ever stops here. The one you came out on, and they wouldn't consider it. The captain is a friend of McKinzie's and is on his payroll. All other boats steer clear of this place. People around here don't take kindly to McKinzie's way of hunting. He's had friends out here and the shooting's been pretty wild. A number of local boats have been hit and there's been a lot of near misses.''

"There must be some way.'' Henry Matthews always said that everyone has his price. Sometimes you just have to meet it. He knew how Mr. Matthews would handle this. "Suppose I let him make his own deal, set his own price for Sandy. He'd have as big a profit as he wanted. Then he could find another cougar. He's a businessman. Wouldn't it give him a great feeling to make such a good deal?''

"Ordinarily yes. But not in this case. As I told you, McKinzie already has his millions. You can't tempt him with money. There's just one thing he'd be sure to go for.''

"What's that?''

"You touched on it a minute ago. Another cougar. But it would have to be one as big or bigger than Sandy. I've no idea where you'd find one. Sandy's the biggest I've ever seen. McKenzie's been wanting one like him for more than two years. He's not about to give him up now.

"Incidentally, you and Sandy were lucky this morning. The launch, on its way back to the mainland, took McKenzie around to the other side of the island to hunt. It saved him a long walk. Otherwise he'd have passed the rock pile and probably shot into it, and Sandy would have come running out. McKinzie could have run smack into you coming here, too.''

"I forgot he might shoot into the cave again."

"Just remember, you won't be this lucky again."

"I'll remember. Can't you think of anything that will help Sandy?"

Ironwood shook his head. "Believe me, the best thing you can do is go back to your folks and forget Sandy. He's as good as dead. There's not a chance of saving him."

"I can't leave him," Paul said. How could he explain to this sharp-eyed little man that Sandy was more than just a tame cougar who was facing death at a hunter's rifle. He was a symbol. Sandy was all the friends he'd not been allowed to have, the pets he'd yearned for and had to pass by. Sandy was the only living thing that had ever put complete trust in him, that had obeyed Paul's every word even when its life was at stake, that depended upon him completely.

"I had a dog once," Ironwood said. "No human has ever meant as much to me as that mutt did. But what about your folks? According to the papers, radio and television, they're mighty worried."

"I have to stay," Paul said simply. "I can't let Sandy face McKinzie alone. Somebody's got to be on his side. If I left I'd always remember that I ran out on him when I could have stayed and maybe done something. I guess," he finished lamely, "I just have to do what I have to."

The black eyes of the Indian searched the blue eyes of the boy. Finally Ironwood looked down at his hands. "That dog of mine wasn't much," he said quietly. "He was just an ugly, bone-headed mutt that wasn't good for anything but getting in people's way and eating like you wouldn't believe. I remember somebody once asked me what kind of dog he was and I said, 'a darn good dog.' And for me he was.

"In my family I was the runt of the litter and the youngest to boot. My three brothers and two sisters were all bigger, better looking, and I'm sure a lot smarter than I was. I was even the runt among my friends. The one chosen last in any game. I was a nothing to everybody but that dog. He loved me, depended on me for his food, bed, and to keep other dogs from chewing him up. And I did. With him I was important, strong, sure of myself. He made me feel big inside. I was about fifteen when he was run over. The day he was killed all those fine things inside me seemed to die."

"That's exactly it," Paul said. "I feel the same way with Sandy. If I walk away and McKinzie kills him . . ." He shook his head. "Those things that died in you I'm trying to keep alive in me. I have to try to save Sandy to do that."

"I guess maybe you do," Ironwood agreed. "You're a pretty brave boy."

"No, I'm not. When bullets started flying around inside the cave yesterday, I was as afraid as Sandy."

"Only a fool wouldn't have been afraid." Ironwood scowled at the floor as if making up his mind about something. Finally he slapped his palms together and said, "All right. I'll help you and Sandy all I can. But I've got to tell you my help won't be much. Don't get your hopes up. As far as I can see all you're going to do is postpone the inevitable. But we'll meet that when we come to it. Now then, number one, you've got to keep out of McKinzie's and Frost's sight if you're going to help Sandy. If either one sees you or even begins to suspect there's somebody else on the island besides them and me it'll be the end of everything."

"What will they do?"

"Hunt you down."

"Hunt me down?"

"Just to get you out of here. You could be hurt accidentally, a fall or something. McKinzie, being a wealthy man, is very fearful of lawsuits. He'd want you off the island for that reason if no other. Also, he and Frost would figure out who you are in jig time. They both pay a lot of attention to newspapers, radio and television.

"If they couldn't find you in a hurry McKinzie would have the state police in here. After all, this is private property and you're a trespasser. So remember, both you and Sandy have got to stay out of sight. And don't leave a lot of footprints in soggy places, or empty cans or paper sacks lying around to give you away. And don't carve blazes on trees for directions. Don't do anything that might start them thinking there's anyone else around. And above all, don't ever light a fire. The flames can be seen even through dense brush, and the smoke from any part of the island."

"I'll be very careful," Paul promised.

"You've got to be. Now then, do you have a pretty

97

good idea of Sandy's habits? I've seen him at odd times but not enough to form a clear picture."

"He sleeps about half the morning up in the cave," Paul said. "He likes to prowl some in the early afternoon. He sleeps again until evening, then wanders around all night."

"About how I had him figured. It's a logical pattern for a cat. You don't have to worry about McKinzie hunting him at night. With that bum leg he's afraid of tripping and falling. So, at night you can let Sandy prowl. When he returns in the morning you've got to keep him with you all day. That's the time McKinzie will be hunting.

"Both of you keep out of the cave during the day. That's an ideal spot for a cat to lay up. When they can't find Sandy, one of them will eventually climb up for a look. So each morning, early, you and Sandy get out. Take everything with you that might give away your presence."

"How can I control Sandy?"

"I'll get you a collar and chain."

"But he's too big and strong. I couldn't hold him."

"You did when McKinzie was shooting into the cave, and he was scared to death. Don't forget, he was raised from a kitten by a man. He's well trained. He's used to being led around on a leash. Once you get a collar and chain on him you'll have no trouble. Come on, I'll fix you up."

Ironwood took Paul up to his small quarters at the back of the lodge. There he had a number of chains and collars and halters hanging from nails on the wall. "All belonged to some animal brought out here to shoot," he explained. He took down a chain and collar and handed it to Paul. "This was worn by a rare goat brought here from Asia or someplace. Put this on Sandy when he returns from his night's prowling, keep him with you all day and let him go again at night. Now, how are you fixed for food?"

"I've got one can of sardines, one ham and five slices of bread left. There's plenty of meat on the haunch."

"You've got enough for today. I'll sneak more up to you tomorrow forenoon. Don't come to the lodge again."

"McKinzie or Frost could spot you bringing us food, or miss the food you bring," Paul pointed out.

"They won't miss the food. I'm the only one that goes into the food cache. I do the cooking. As for spotting me on the trail," he smiled, "I'm an Indian. Just be sure to keep Sandy out of the cave during the day. The back side of the rock pile has some good hiding places. Find a depression, a lot of jagged rocks where the going will be tough for anyone looking for you, one with plenty of brush around it.

"Won't they look all over the rock pile?"

"Not likely. The back part is hard to get to from the ground; also it's not a logical place for a cat to hang out. The cave is. I think they'll look there and let the rest go."

"How will you find us?"

"I'll find you," Ironwood smiled. "I'll be up most

every morning. I'll bring grub and tell you what part of the island McKinzie plans to hunt. But don't go wandering around in daylight, even if you've got a good reason. Another thing, you're on the tip of the island now. No matter where McKinzie hunts he'll pass the rock pile. The kind of man he is, you can figure he'll shoot into the cave about every time he passes."

"I'll do whatever you say, and thanks."

"I like Sandy, too. He's the one needs the help. You can go back any time you like." Ironwood scratched his chin thoughtfully. "Maybe I'm doing this a little bit for myself, too. When I ran out on my problem I lost a lot of my own self-respect. Maybe this will help me get a little of it back.

"Just you remember one thing. Time is on their side, not ours. Eventually something's bound to blow our cover."

"Like what?" Paul asked.

Ironwood shrugged. "Maybe McKinzie or Frost will just naturally become suspicious if they can't find Sandy. Then they'll start an inch-by-inch search that's bound to flush both of you out. There's also your folks. You can't be gone much longer. The hunt for you is getting hotter by the day." Ironwood shook his head, "There's an awful lot stacked against us and nothing going for us. All we can hope to do is go along the next couple of days and wait for whatever's going to happen.

"Now you'd better get back to Sandy before he wakes and begins to prowl again." As Paul turned to leave he cautioned, "Keep your eyes open on the way back. McKinzie's supposed to be hunting the opposite side of the island, but you can never tell about that man.''

Paul hurried along the trail carrying the chain and collar. He approached each bend and blind spot in the trail cautiously, but nothing happened. He crossed the little glade and climbed the rocks to the cave.

Sandy was gone.

Paul's first reaction was to go looking for him. But the cat traveled fast and could be anywhere. And he might run into McKinzie. He'd have to wait for Sandy to return. "Stay wild, Sandy," he told himself. "Keep out of sight and be careful.''

Paul didn't like staying in the cave during the day, so carrying the collar and chain, he climbed to the flat rock above where he could command a view of the surrounding forest and the distant sea. It was warm and pleasant on the rock. He could see but not be seen.

He had been there about an hour. The day was utterly still and he was dozing when two spaced shots floated down the slight breeze from the direction McKinzie was supposed to be hunting. He sat up and listened. There were no more shots.

Those shots had been deliberate, careful. The marksman had taken plenty of time to be sure of his target. He kept visualizing Sandy as he remembered him, lying warm and soft against his legs, the sleepy, satisfied sound of his purring, the silky feel of his fur and the soft warmth of his tongue licking his cheek. He'd never forget the trembling of his body, the moaning fright when McKinzie shot into the cave. He remembered how Sandy walked the trail last night, a step ahead, as if leading the way.

Paul thought of McKinzie, cold, impersonal, the dedicated killer. Those shots, spaced as they were, meant one thing. He had lost the only real friend he'd ever had. He would never feel quite the same again.

8

Paul sat on top of the rock a long time. He tried not to think of Sandy and what had happened. It had to be Sandy, he told himself. There was no other big game on the island. If McKinzie shot at a squirrel or rabbit the sound would have frightened Sandy. So he'd save his shooting for the cat.

The sun climbed the sky until it was straight overhead. The heat of the day bore down upon him. Beneath him the world lay still and almost breathless. In the distance a white fishing boat moved slowly across the sea.

Paul kept telling himself that as long as it was over he might as well return to the lodge and let them take him back to the mainland. But he continued to sit. He wasn't sure why.

He didn't hear Sandy climbing up the rock pile. But suddenly he was rubbing his head against Paul and purring at the top of his lungs. Paul put an arm around his neck and said, "Where have you been? Don't you know

McKinzie's out looking for you to kill you? You darned fool. You've got to be more careful. You had me worried sick. Was old Limpy McKinzie shooting at you or something else?'' Sandy yawned luxuriously, flopped on his side and put a paw over his eyes.

Paul fastened the collar around his neck and snapped the chain to it. ''From now on you're through rambling around in the daylight.''

Sandy thumped the black tip of his tail on the rock and promptly went to sleep.

Paul wrapped the end of the chain around his hand, lay back on the rock beside the cat and closed his eyes. In a short time he, too, slept.

Sandy tugging on the chain awoke Paul. The cat was standing, looking down into the little glade.

Paul glanced down. The glade was empty. ''Nothing doing,'' he said. ''You don't go rambling off anymore during the day.'' This was the test he'd worried about. If Sandy decided to go he couldn't possibly hold him.

Paul remembered he'd once heard an animal trainer say that part of the secret of controlling a wild animal was to speak with authority. He made his voice sound as commanding as possible and said, ''You come back here and lie down. Come on, Sandy. Lie down.'' He tugged on the chain and patted the rock beside him.

Sandy looked at him, blinking yellow eyes, seeming to be making up his mind.

''Come on,'' Paul commanded. ''Now.'' Sandy padded to Paul and lay down. Paul patted his head and said, ''Good boy. That's a good boy.''

They stayed there and watched the sun slip down the sky. First shadows crept through the trees and across the glade. A breeze came off the sea. The heat of the day began to leave. The sun sank beneath the treetops. Then Paul rose and said, "All right, let's go back to the cave and get something to eat." Sandy followed, obedient as any dog as they picked their way down over the rocks.

In the cave they shared a can of ham and Paul ate two slices of bread. Afterward they sat outside on the ledge and watched the sun drop from sight. The shadows deepened and night closed down. Sandy began to pace the length of the chain.

Paul said, "I guess it's safe now. I'll turn you loose as soon as I've had a drink." They picked their way down the face of the rock and went along the trail to the little spring. There they both drank; then Paul unsnapped the chain and watched Sandy fade silently into the night.

Paul returned to the cave, made himself comfortable against the wall and settled down to sleep. In the city it would still be early. People would be getting ready to go out for the evening. He wondered what his parents were doing.

When Paul awoke gray dawn was lighting the cave and Sandy had returned. Paul snapped the chain to his collar and patted his shoulder. "You're pretty smart. You got back early."

He searched the inside of the cave for something to fasten the chain to. The walls were smooth. But he found a big crack toward the back. He could wedge a stick in there and tie the chain to it. He went outside to look for a stick. Down below, at the edge of the glade, several big limbs were lying on the ground. He climbed down, broke about four feet off one and returned to the cave. He wedged the stick into the crack in such a way it could be removed only by lifting it up. He tied the chain to it, gave it a couple of experimental tugs and was satisfied it would hold Sandy.

He made himself a sandwich of the last can of sardines, and stood in the mouth of the cave eating and watching the day advance. When the sun was well up and beginning to warm, he returned inside, and gathered up all the food and the empty sardine can. He looked about carefully, making sure nothing was left to show a human had been here. He untied the chain from the wedged limb and shook Sandy awake. "All right," he said, "let's go find a hiding place." He was surprised how obediently Sandy rose, stretched and yawned, and followed him out of the cave.

They climbed to the top, crossed the flat surface and went down the back side of the rock pile. It was much rougher than the face. In spots it was steeper. Jagged rocks thrust up in all directions. The brush was so thick Paul could hardly push through. About a third of the way down he came into a natural depression about four feet deep by ten square. It was ringed by brush that was impossible to see through. Getting down (or up) here would be torture for McKinzie and hard even for Frost. He tied Sandy's chain to the base of a bush, put the food

106

in the shade of a rock and settled down to wait out the daylight hours.

Sandy flopped in the sun and promptly went back to sleep.

Paul lay on his back in the most comfortable spot he could find and stared up at the cloudless blue bowl of the sky. A single small puffball cloud sailed into the bowl. He watched it out of sight, wondering idly where it would finally go. Once again he thought about his parents, the concert he'd missed, and the police who were looking for him. Then he thought about McKinzie. Paul was wondering what made McKinzie the kind of man he was when he was brought bolt-upright by the crashing sound of a shot. It rolled up from the glade, smashed across the island and died away in echoes. A flock of startled crows flapped away. A pair of small birds nearby fled through the brush in panic.

Sandy was instantly on his feet, yellow eyes sprung wide with fear. Every muscle was tensed to spring. But he was momentarily held by the chain.

Paul grabbed him and whispered, "Down, Sandy. Down! Down!" He pressed the cat to the ground. Sandy crouched on all fours. Again Paul felt the trembling of his muscles. "It's all right," he whispered. "It's all right." His hands stroked reassuringly. He waited the next shot.

It came with the same shattering violence as the first. Even though he was expecting it, he jumped. Sandy began making small moaning sounds. Paul held him down and continued to talk to him.

A third shot finally came.

There were no more. Silence settled over the island again.

After a few minutes Sandy relaxed and stopped trembling. Finally he turned on his side, put a paw over his eyes and calmly went back to sleep.

A little later Joe Ironwood stepped silently into the depression carrying a brown cloth bag. "That cannon makes quite a racket," he observed. He sat down cross-legged and looked about. "Good spot you've got. I was right on it before I saw it. I'm glad you and Sandy were out of the cave. You had no trouble with him on the chain?"

"He handled like a dog."

"Good." Ironwood opened the sack and took out a loaf of bread, some packaged lunch meat and two cans of pork and beans. "On the beans," he explained, "leave the empty cans here. I'll take them back tomorrow. Now, for McKinzie, he'll be hunting this area for a couple of days. Then he'll move over west and take that side of the island. You and Sandy lay low right here. Let Sandy roam all he wants at night. He'll be safe then. Incidentally, I haven't heard him scream the past couple of nights. I figure that's because he's no longer lonesome. He's found a friend. Well, I'd better be getting back."

"What if you run into McKinzie on the trail? Won't he become suspicious?"

"My job's keeping the trails clear. I'm just looking

things over." He pointed at the sleeping Sandy. "Keep his nibs here all day."

He was gone as quietly as he'd come.

Noon came. The sun stood straight overhead. Paul opened one of the cans of beans and ate. Sandy continued to sleep.

In the early afternoon Sandy awoke and tugged experimentally on the chain. He walked a circle at its extreme length. Then he sat down and looked questioningly at Paul.

Paul patted his head. "You want to go roaming around. Well, you can't. You might as well relax."

When the sun fell into the treetops Paul opened the loaf of bread and package of lunchmeat and made himself a sandwich. Afterward he cut slices from the dried haunch and fed Sandy every other one.

Sandy paced the length of the chain until the dying sun threw the shadow of the rock pile across the depression. Paul watched night creep through the trees. When it seemed sufficiently dark, he unsnapped the chain and said, "All right, go ahead. I guess it's safe now. Just be sure you get back early in the morning."

Sandy was gone almost immediately.

Paul gathered up the chain and food, returned to the cave and left them inside. Then he climbed down the rock pile and made his way along the trail to the spring and had his first good drink of the day. "I'm as bad as Sandy," he thought. "I can't go out in the daylight either."

Back at the cave he sat outside and listened to the night come alive like an orchestra tuning up. Eventually a cool breeze drove him inside. He made himself comfortable against the wall and almost immediately fell asleep.

When he woke, Sandy was stretched out beside him. This time he didn't wait. He snapped the chain to the cougar's collar, gathered up the food and said, "Come on, Sandy. Let's get out of here."

They climbed to the top and went down the rough back side to the depression. After he tied the chain to a bush, Paul hacked open a can of beans and opened the loaf of bread. Sandy went back to sleep.

They had been there about an hour when the first shot thundered into the silence. Again Paul held Sandy down. But he did not seem as frightened this time.

Some minutes after the last shot, Ironwood stepped into the depression and sat down. He had the brown sack again, and from it he extracted a chunk of cake and two cans of peaches. "I hear McKinzie was here. You know, any ordinary person would quit that shooting into the cave. After doing it a couple of times he'd figure the cat wasn't there. Not McKinzie. He's a bullhead."

"Sandy wasn't as frightened as usual. I guess he's getting used to the noise."

"More likely it's you. He expects you to take care of him. He trusts you." He leaned back and smiled at Paul. "McKinzie's beginning to get a little uptight," he said cheerfully. "He's been hunting Sandy four days and hasn't seen hide nor hair of him."

"Are you sure?"

"Dead sure. I've watched this man for months. I know the signs. And McKinzie getting uptight is getting to Frost, too. His job depends on keeping McKinzie happy. He's not happy now."

"Does that mean McKinzie might give up?" Paul asked hopefully.

Ironwood shook his head, "It means he's a very impatient man. He should have bagged Sandy in two days at most, the very most. It annoys him. Like a lot of successful men, he wants everything to happen yesterday. He has very little patience. I can guarantee he won't tramp these trails much longer. He'll do something to force the issue."

"Like what?"

"Who knows. With his kind of money he can do any number of things. To name a few, he might hire a helicopter to fly over the island and try to spot Sandy from the air. He could bring in more men and comb every inch of the island, or bring in tracking dogs, or put out baits. One thing I am sure of—he won't be satisfied just shooting into that cave much longer. He knows it's a perfect place for a cat. Either he or Frost will eventually climb up for a look-see. So be sure you're not there during the day, and don't leave a single scrap of anything lying around that will give you away."

"I'll be careful. You said bait. What kind of bait?"

"My guess is a goat or maybe a sheep. Something

that will draw Sandy to a spot where McKinzie will be waiting. If he does that, you'll have to keep Sandy on the chain night and day.''

''If he can't find him then will he quit?''

Ironwood shook his head. ''Not that man. If one thing doesn't work, he'll try another. He knows Sandy's here someplace. Whatever he does we've got to counter it. So far, so good. Where's those empty bean cans? I'd better get back.''

Paul and Sandy spent the day in the depression. Sandy slept until late afternoon. Paul napped briefly. With the coming of evening, Paul ate and fed Sandy; then they climbed to the cave, left the food and went to the spring. Both drank, after which Paul turned Sandy loose and watched him lose himself almost immediately.

At the cave Paul watched the stars come out. A fat moon rode into view, sailing grandly over the treetops. So McKinzie was annoyed and uptight after the fourth day of fruitless hunting. Today was the fifth. He didn't doubt Ironwood when he said the big lumberman would do something to force the issue. He wondered what it would be, and when McKinzie would do it.

They were in the depression the next morning and Paul was waiting for the sound of the rifle when Ironwood arrived.

''There hasn't been any shooting yet,'' Paul said. ''He's late.''

''There won't be any. There's been a change in the hunting technique. Remember I told you McKinzie wouldn't tramp these trails hunting Sandy much longer because he's an impatient man? Well, Frost knows it, too. He's worried. He's talked McKinzie into putting out baits to hurry it up.''

"What kind of bait?"

"Catnip."

"That's bait?"

"One of the best. Cats love it. They can smell it more than a quarter of a mile away. It's a big bunch of catnip fastened to a fir tree alongside the trail to the lodge. Frost knows Sandy walked that trail a lot. The catnip is behind a square of tin that's punched full of holes and nailed to the tree about two feet off the ground. Frost put a platform in another tree some thirty yards away. McKinzie is probably sitting up there now waiting for Sandy. There's a ladder leaning against the tree so McKinzie can go up and down. Don't let Sandy loose tonight. Keep a tight leash on him twenty-four hours a day."

"McKinzie's going to stay up there day and night?"

"No. But if Sandy runs loose tonight he'll head for the tree. You might not be able to get him to leave. Catnip's like a drug. Cats go a little crazy when they get around it."

Ironwood rummaged in the sack. "I brought a chunk of raw meat for Sandy so he won't go hungry." Ironwood rose to leave. "Keep him on the chain until I tell you to let him loose. Don't feed him until evening. He probably caught something during the night and isn't hungry now anyway. If you feed him at sundown he won't be quite so restless tonight. Incidentally," he added, "they've come to the conclusion you've been kidnapped. They're waiting for ransom demands."

Paul thought about that after Ironwood left. He was sorry to put his folks through this suspense, but it couldn't be helped. They'd be that much happier when they saw him.

Paul waited until evening to feed Sandy. He cut the chunk of raw meat in two and gave Sandy half. Then he gathered up all his stuff and, leading the cat, climbed to the cave. He left the food and, with Sandy, went down the face of the rock pile and along the trail to the spring.

They both drank. Then Sandy showed his restlessness to take off and prowl. Paul took a short grip on the chain and said, "Nothing doing. You're going back to the cave with me." Sandy pulled back but Paul yanked on the chain and said impatiently, "Come on. I'm trying to save your life. Can't you get that through your thick head?"

Sandy finally dropped in beside him and allowed Paul to lead him back to the cave. There Paul tied the chain to the piece of limb and wedged it into the crack in the rock. But Sandy would not settle down. He paced the dark interior of the cave for hours.

Next morning Paul fed Sandy the other half of the chunk of raw meat, after which he gathered up everything and they picked their way down the rock pile to the depression.

Ironwood came silently, as always, startling Paul with his sudden appearance. Again he brought a huge chunk of raw meat for Sandy and prepared sandwiches this time for Paul.

"McKinzie's getting pretty edgy," he said. "He stayed up on that platform till way after dark last night. When he came in he was in a foul mood. He's trying it again today. If it doesn't work Frost is going to change the bait."

"What next?"

"A big red rooster. He'll stake him out on a string in the middle of the trail near the platform and catnip tree. That rooster's crowing will be heard all over the island. So be sure you keep Sandy on the chain."

"Joe," Paul asked, "how much longer?"

"You getting tired? You want to quit?"

"I'm tired," Paul confessed. "I'd like to quit. But I won't until I've saved Sandy. Will we go through this again tomorrow, and the next day and the next?"

"I don't know. You saved Sandy yesterday. You're saving him today. Tomorrow I don't know. I told you how this would be."

"I know."

"It's not like singing, is it?"

Paul shook his head. "Once the concert's over the pressure's off."

"And this is like practicing and practicing and no concert?"

"Yes."

115

Ironwood's black eyes studied Paul, noting the lines of strain around his mouth and eyes. "You're quite a fighter," he said.

"I've never had a fight."

"Trying to accomplish something against odds is fighting. It's refusing to quit when the chips are stacked against you. You're in two of the biggest fights of your life right now. You're trying to save Sandy and make a place for yourself in the sun. You've got a lot of opposition but you haven't quit." He picked up a stick and idly broke it. "I quit," he said.

"How do you mean?"

"Remember I told you I had a problem similar to yours, and I walked away from it? Mine was my family and my people. There's a lot of poverty on the reservation and for most of us there's no way out. We have to pull ourselves up by our bootstraps. We've got two important assets—scads of beautiful timber and a fine resort spot. I worked out a scheme to start a sawmill and develop the resort location. It would have put most of the people to work and brought in a handsome income. I even had financing all worked out. But they laughed at me."

"Laughed at you?"

"Might as well have. All the time I was explaining it to them, I could see they were thinking of that bandy-legged runt. The one who was always chosen last in any game. They gave my plans the same consideration they'd given me as a kid. Boy, did I feel it. I walked out in a huff when I should have stayed and fought like you're doing. The odds wouldn't have been as big as yours are."

"You can go back."

"I intend to, as soon as you and Sandy are taken care of. I figure if you, a kid not yet dry behind the ears, who knows nothing about animals and the wild, can put up this kind of battle against two grown men like Frost and McKinzie, I can make my people listen to me. And I'm not even including the battle with your folks and manager, which I know is a big one." He rose and stood grinning down at Paul. "Whether you save Sandy or not, you're going to help me get back some of my self-respect. Well, I'd better get back. Don't forget, keep Sandy with you."

"Should we stay out of the cave? There's been no shooting for two days. McKinzie's sitting on that platform watching the bait."

"Stay out of the cave during the day. Like I told you, McKinzie's unpredictable."

After Ironwood had gone Paul lay on his back, looked up at the blue sky and thought of the little Indian's words. Ironwood thought he was a fighter. He didn't feel like one. He was deadly tired, and a night's sleep didn't seem to help. He was getting jittery. The pressure was building and building, like it did the last seconds behind the curtain while he waited to walk out. Once onstage it left. Here it built and built. There was no release. He wondered how much longer he could take it.

9

The voice of the rooster rode sharp and clear through the morning stillness. Paul stood in the cave entrance eating a sandwich, listening. There was no doubt the sound could be heard all over the island. He glanced back into the cave. Sandy was on his feet straining at the end of the chain. His ears were pricked forward, yellow eyes expectant, tail snapping.

"Not a chance," Paul said. "If you got down there it'd be sure death." He fed Sandy part of the meat Ironwood brought yesterday, then gathered up the rest of the food and led Sandy out the cave and down the back side of the rock pile to the depression. The rooster crowed twice during their passage. Each time Sandy wanted to turn that way. Paul had to yank on the chain and scold to keep him coming.

Ironwood arrived an hour later. He brought more food and reported that McKinzie was out very early sitting on the platform in the tree. "He's pinning all his hopes on that rooster bringing Sandy right to him."

"Sandy would like to go." Paul told him the trouble he had that morning. "McKinzie would have killed him already if he was loose."

"Frost is betting everything on the rooster," Ironwood said. "If he don't bring Sandy to the gun, he's in trouble with McKinzie, and he knows it. This is the first time McKinzie hasn't bagged his trophy within a few hours or a day or at most two. Well, it's Alec Frost's problem. He'll have to figure a way out. I'm leaving here as soon as this is over."

"I'm glad," Paul said.

"So am I. Watch his nibs here close. If he gets loose he'll make right for that squawking rooster and nothing will stop him."

Sandy was restless most of the day. The rooster's crows diminished in number, but they still came often enough to keep him up and pacing back and forth at the end of the chain. He did not settle down until it was dark again and the rooster had quieted down for the night. Paul was afraid he might have trouble with the cat when they went to the spring, but Sandy paced along as usual. He even allowed himself to be led back to the cave with only minor objections.

Ironwood was all smiles when he arrived next morning. "Good news," he said. "The best. McKinzie is plenty upset because he hasn't seen hide nor hair of Sandy.

The catnip didn't work. The rooster didn't work yesterday and he could be heard all over the island."

"What does that mean?"

"I've never seen McKinzie as upset as he was last night. He takes his hunting mighty serious. He tore into Frost last night, demanding to know what had happened to his cat. As if it was all Frost's fault. But that's McKinzie for you. Anyway, Frost couldn't tell him. In a way I felt kind of sorry for the man. He did a good job making Sandy wild. I even got called into it."

"How?"

"Frost tried to explain things and defend himself, but it did no good. I happened to be in the room." Ironwood smiled slyly. "I've made a habit of being around close lately, where I can hear—in case something is said that could be important to us.

"Well, McKinzie said, 'Joe, if Frost got that cat wild, like he claims, what happened to him? You're an Indian. You know about these things.' I don't, but I acted wise anyway.

"I said, 'Alec did a good job getting Sandy wild with his close shooting. Maybe he did too good a job.'

"'What do you mean, too good a job?' Frost demanded. 'I was supposed to get him wild. I did.'

"I said, 'We used to hear him scream almost every night, remember? We haven't heard him once in almost a week. There's no sign of him, no nothing. This island's not very big. That rooster can be heard all over it, and the catnip can be smelled over half of it. Both are irresistible to cats. But he didn't show. He's disappeared like he never was.'

" 'What're you driving at?' McKinzie wanted to know.

" 'I think he's gone,' I said.

" 'Gone where?' McKinzie asked. 'You said the island's not big, and it's ten miles to the mainland. Are you suggesting somebody took him off in a boat or something? If they did I'll run them down if it's the last thing I do.'

" 'I think he tried to swim to the mainland,' I said. 'He knew he had to cross the water to get home. The homing instinct in a cat is mighty strong. I think he tried it rather than face any more shooting at him. I think the rifle scared him that much.'

" 'If he tried that swim he drowned,' McKinzie said.

" 'That's what I think,' I told him.

" 'I can't go along with that,' McKinzie said. 'Even an animal's got more sense than to try a ten-mile swim.'

" 'I've seen cornered deer jump off a hundred-foot bluff rather than face dogs or a man,' I said."

"You have?" Paul asked.

"No." Ironwood smiled. "But he don't know that. Alec Frost was annoyed with me for hinting that Sandy was dead and said, 'Come on, Joe, don't try to push that old Apache legend off on us.'

" 'Legend,' McKinzie said. 'What legend?'

"I'd heard about it when I was a kid. Since Frost brought it up, I thought, why not use it? You never know what's going to help. So I said, 'There's an old Apache legend that says when you hear a cougar scream somebody's going to die.'

" 'You go for legends, Joe?' McKinzie asked.

"I said, 'All I know for sure is the cat's gone. I say he's dead.'

"McKinzie shook his head. 'I don't go for legends, or any other hocus-pocus. Everything's got a logical explanation including this cat's disappearance. I want to know what it is. If he tried to swim to the mainland, he drowned. But I don't see any animal committing suicide. He couldn't help knowing it was too long a swim. Why, you can't even see any land to swim to. The only other thing—somebody took him off.' He looked at Frost and then at me.

"Alec Frost said, 'Why would I? I got him for you to begin with. Give me one reason.'

"McKinzie looked at me and I said, 'I'm just the caretaker. What you do with these animals doesn't mean a thing to me.'

" 'Then I've got to assume he's still here,' McKinzie said, 'and I've missed him somehow. What about bringing in a sheep? Cougars like sheep.'

"Frost said, 'I can call Captain Edwards. He can bring out a sheep. But he can't get it here before sometime late tomorrow. That means another day. I might point out, Mr. McKinzie, cats like chicken about as well as sheep. That rooster's crow can be heard all over the island. A sheep's bleat can't.'

" 'He's right,' I agreed, hoping to cut one more day

off the hunt. 'A rooster's crow will draw that cat more than a sheep if he's around to hear it.'

"McKinzie scowled. He don't like being contradicted. But he finally said, 'All right. I'll go with the rooster another day. If we don't find the cat tomorrow, then he's not here, and I'm through chasing around this island for nothing.' "

Ironwood spread his hands and smiled. "So, there you are, my fighting friend. Today's the day."

"Then we've saved Sandy! We've saved him, Joe!" Paul wanted to jump and yell at the top of his lungs. "We've saved him! We've really saved him! Old McKinzie loses. Doesn't he, Joe?"

"Hold your horses," Ironwood said calmly. "Just hold everything."

"But McKinzie said one more day. That means he's quitting tonight, doesn't it?"

"I hope so. But not necessarily. Remember I told you he's as unpredictable as the wind. He gets his own way in all things, and he's always dead sure he's right. Above all, he doesn't like to get beaten, and he's getting beaten now. He's a cold-blooded killer who shoots anything that crawls, runs, swims or flies."

"So?"

"So he can change his mind. He can decide to try another day, and another. Once before that I know of, he had trouble running down a trophy and threatened to quit, then changed his mind, went out and got it. He could do it again. So don't get excited yet. There's still today and who knows what after that. You and Sandy

123

lay low. We've still got a way to go. The odds are still against us, and they're getting less, but not enough less to say we've won. However, we can do a little planning now—just in case. I always like to be prepared for any eventuality.''

"All right. What do we do?''

"If McKinzie really calls it quits tonight we've got to have him and Frost off the island so we can get Sandy away from here. McKinzie always leaves as soon as he's through hunting. He's too restless to hang around doing nothing. In all probability Frost will go out on the launch with him to shop for more animals, or supplies, or something. That'll leave me here alone. We've got shortwave here. I'll call a man I know on the mainland who has a fast thirty-foot boat. He'll come out, take you and Sandy off, and nobody will ever know. The boat can cost you as much as a hundred dollars.''

"That's great,'' Paul said. "It's just what I want. Where can I take Sandy?''

"You said you wanted to turn him loose. You can't do that on the mainland. He'd head for home. A good place would be Skull Island.''

"Where's that?''

"About twenty miles further out to sea. It's big: about fifteen or twenty miles long by five or six wide, and completely wild. Nobody lives there. It's overrun with wild game of all kinds.''

"Sandy would be safe?''

"Absolutely. Nobody goes out there even to hunt. It's not only very rough, it was once an Indian burial

124

ground. That's how it got its name. Everybody steers clear of it.''

"It sounds great. You think McKinzie will leave tomorrow?''

"Whoa, I didn't say anything like that. It is a remote possibility—if he's completely frustrated again today, and he feels tonight as he did last night, he might. Don't forget all this is conjecture. The odds are no better than fifty-fifty at best. I'm not counting on anything. I just want to have some kind of plan should things break our way. I never expected anything like this might happen. It's almost too good to be true—if it happens, that is. I've a sneaking suspicion he's very anxious to get back. He has many business interests, and he's been gone longer this time than usual. Anyway, I'll slip out tomorrow and keep you posted.''

"Can I turn Sandy loose tonight? He's getting mighty restless.''

"Absolutely not. Keep him on the chain. But there's no reason to come down here tomorrow. You might as well stay in the cave. I'll contact you there. Maybe you'd better try to get a little extra sleep. You look like you could use it. If all goes well, day after tomorrow at the latest, you can be with your folks, and his nibs here will be safe on a big island all his own.''

"I hope so,'' Paul said.

As Ironwood was about to leave, Paul asked, "Joe, is there really an Apache legend about a cougar screaming and somebody dying?''

"There's the legend.''

"Do you believe it?"

Ironwood shrugged. "Something had to happen to start the legend. I've known of some mighty odd happenings that can't be explained. Who can say, for dead sure, what's fact and what isn't?"

With that he left.

Paul lay back, looked up at the sky and smiled. He wanted to run and shout until he dropped. He squinted at the bright sun and said softly, "How are you this fine day, Mr. Sun?" Beside him Sandy slept peacefully, a paw over his eyes, as if nothing earth-shaking had happened.

The tension of the past days began to let go. Paul was tired. Looking back he wondered how he had made it to here. In spite of Ironwood's warnings, he felt they were going to win over McKinzie. It would be good to return to his parents, to begin preparing for the next concert. They would be treating him differently from now on. He didn't see how he could wait even one more day.

A thing had taken place last night after Frost, Ironwood and McKinzie talked, that the Indian knew nothing of.

Frost had gone immediately to his room, where the shortwave radio was housed, and put in a call for Captain Edwards aboard the launch *Wanderer* lying at the dock on the mainland. McKinzie's disappointment over losing his cougar trophy worried Frost. He knew the big lumberman's temperament. He could not tolerate frustration or failure, and now he was faced with both. He would take out his anger on someone. Right or wrong that someone would be Alec Frost. McKinzie would consider that he had failed. He'd been hired to do a job and had not produced. McKinzie wouldn't hesitate to fire him and get a new gamekeeper.

Frost doubted that another day's hunting would bag Sandy. He was baffled by the big cat's disappearance. He was inclined to agree with Joe Ironwood that somehow the cat had gotten off the island. Maybe he had tried to swim to the mainland and drowned. He didn't dare admit that to McKinzie.

The lumberman's reputation, wealth, appearance and bearing awed Frost. He never crossed McKinzie. He was always thinking ahead for things he could do that would keep him in the man's good graces. At the moment he desperately needed a good substitute to take McKinzie's mind off his loss of Sandy, if, as he was afraid, tomorrow turned up nothing. He was sure he had just what it would take.

McKinzie once mentioned that he'd like to kill a European fallow deer. Frost had begun searching for one weeks ago. By great good fortune he learned of a Persian fallow deer at a game farm no more than a hundred miles away. The farm was in financial trouble. The deer could be bought. Frost made a special trip to see the animal.

The deer was in good condition. It was not as wild as he'd like. But McKinzie would never know the difference. It was silvery, almost white in color, and it carried a good rack of horns. He made a substantial down payment and left the deer there until he should send for it.

Frost never told McKinzie or Ironwood about the deer. That was his job insurance against a mishap such as he was afraid was about to happen. Now he needed it.

Frost had no trouble raising Captain Edwards aboard the *Wanderer*. He told him about the fallow deer and where it could be found. "Get in touch with them immediately, tonight," he said. "Have them fly the animal out to the coast to you tomorrow. You bring it to the island. I've got to have that animal on the island by tomorrow night."

"Good enough," Captain·Edwards said. "It'll be there."

With that Frost crawled into bed. Not to sleep, to lie scowling at the ceiling, wondering what had happened to Sandy.

10

At dusk George McKinzie climbed stiffly down from the lookout platform in the fir tree. He was hungry, tired and thirsty. His bad leg ached from the unnatural position he had assumed. He stood a minute rubbing the pain out of the leg and scowling sourly at the rooster busily scratching in the trail a few feet away and talking to himself. Finally McKinzie took a knife from his pocket, got hold of the string and pulled the rooster to him, complaining loudly. He cut the string. "Go ahead, get out of here," he grumbled. "You're no good to me." He watched the rooster trot off down the trail, still complaining to himself. Then he turned toward the lodge.

He was angry, annoyed, and frustrated. He'd wasted a week hunting this cat and hadn't seen a sign of him. He had wanted such a trophy for a long time. He might never find another cat as big. He'd had the animal within his grasp; then it had disappeared into thin air.

Maybe Ironwood was right. The cat had tried to swim the miles to the mainland. What was that crazy Indian superstition? When the cougar screams somebody is going to die. It looked like this cat had.

McKinzie had the prying kind of mind that wouldn't leave a problem alone. He did not like mysteries and he was not superstitious. The cat had to be mighty frightened to try that swim—if he had. He certainly hadn't done anything to scare it. Neither had Ironwood. Frost was the one who had deliberately frightened the cat. He was struck by a thought that stopped him dead in the trail. Frost had made the cat wild by shooting close to it. Maybe he'd accidentally killed it and was afraid to admit it, or crippled it and it crawled off somewhere and died. That made sense.

McKinzie was suddenly angry. Frost had made a fool of him, letting him run around here for days hunting a cat that he knew was already dead. If Frost thought he was going to get away with a fast one like that he had another think coming. He started off, swinging the stiff leg angrily.

Frost and Ironwood were in the big room when he arrived. Ironwood was laying a fire in the fireplace. Frost was cleaning a rifle.

Frost said matter-of-factly, "You didn't see him."

"You know I didn't." McKinzie's voice had an edge. He leaned the rifle in a corner and faced Frost.

Frost squinted down the cleaned barrel. "If you'd seen him there'd been shots. There weren't any."

McKinzie said in a flat voice, "The cat's dead. You knew it before I came out here."

Frost laid the rifle down carefully. "What are you talking about, Mr. McKinzie?"

"It didn't make sense, that cat trying to swim ten miles to the mainland, just because he was scared of a little rifle fire. And it doesn't make sense that on this small island I can't find him now. I should have figured what happened after the second day."

"I'm not following you," Frost said. "What do you figure happened?"

"I'll spell it out plain. You told me you shot at the cat to make him wild. Well, you killed him. Oh, it was an accident. But you killed him. Then you let me come out here and go ramming around for days like some kind of fool amateur hunter, because you didn't have the nerve to admit it. You figured I'd fire you if I knew the truth. And you were dead right."

Frost was violently shaking his head. "No. No, that's not how it was at all. It was just like I told you. I never touched that cat with a bullet. I hit what I aim at. I'm a dead shot. You know I am. I've done this very same thing for you with half a dozen other animals and I never touched one of them."

"Accidents happen," McKinzie said coldly. "Maybe you didn't hit the cat directly. The bullet ricocheted off a rock or something, struck the cat and crippled him. He crawled off someplace and died. One way or another I figure you had to kill that cat. What I can't excuse is

131

letting me chase around here looking like a fool for days, wasting valuable time.''

Frost kept shaking his head. ''It's just like I told you, Mr. McKinzie. Exactly. If I'd killed him accidentally I'd have told you because you'd have figured it out somehow. You ask Joe how it was. He was here the whole time. Every day. Ask him.''

''He's right,'' Ironwood said. ''I saw the cat a number of times. He was fine. Alec did a good job getting him wild. I didn't see him the last day or so. That's when I figure he couldn't take it anymore. I still say he tried that swim to the mainland. I don't find it surprising. In fact, there's a snapshot hanging in your room that you took yourself of a deer swimming a good mile from one island to another. If a deer will do, why not a cougar? He's a better swimmer.''

McKinzie looked into the steady black eyes of the Indian. He had no reason to doubt Ironwood. He certainly was not worried about his job. Somehow he trusted Ironwood more than he did Frost.

''Well,'' he conceded finally, ''maybe you're right. But it doesn't make much sense—an animal acting like that. I've wasted a week out here without even a rabbit hide to show for it.''

''Maybe it's not completely wasted, Mr. McKinzie,'' Frost said hastily. ''Remember that stag, the European fallow deer you wanted?''

''Stag? Deer?'' McKinzie frowned.

''You showed me a picture of it a few months ago.

You cut it out of a paper. You said you wanted one. He had a fine, big rack of horns and was sort of speckled white.''

"Oh, that. What about it?''

"I've got one for you. Not a European, a Persian fallow deer,'' he said triumphantly. "They're a lot scarcer than the European. It's one of the least-known and rarest of animals.''

"That's fine.'' McKinzie was only half listening. His craggy face showed no pleasure or excitement. "I've been away long enough. I ought to be getting back. Lot of things to catch up on. Maybe some other time.''

Frost rushed on, "This stag is found only along the Persian-Iraqi border. There's between two and four hundred left in the world. They were once thought extinct; then they were found again in 1875. Then they were considered extinct again until a few were found in 1951 along the Persian-Iraqi border.''

McKinzie's scowling face told Frost nothing.

Then he threw his final bit of information at the lumberman. "These few animals are protected like you wouldn't believe. No hunter in North America, maybe not even in the world, is going to bag one—except maybe you. Maybe you, Mr. McKinzie,'' he repeated. "And this is the last chance even you will ever have.''

McKinzie looked at Frost then. "Rare, eh? Nobody else is getting one?''

"That's right, Mr. McKinzie.''

"You're sure it's a Persian fallow deer?''

"Dead sure. I've been looking weeks, ever since you mentioned you wanted one. This could be the only one on a private game farm in the country. I don't know how they came by it. The only reason I could buy it is because the farm is in financial difficulties. What I figured, Mr. McKinzie, is as long as you're here, you could hunt the stag. He can sort of take the place of the cougar."

"Nothing will take the place of that cougar. I had my mind set on him. I still want a big cougar. You keep looking. There must be one around someplace."

"I'll keep looking," Frost promised.

McKinzie's black brows were pulled together, "A Persian fallow deer, huh? Where's he now?"

"Captain Edwards is on the way out with him. He should be here anytime."

"All right. As long as he's on the way out, I'll look at him. I did want one."

A half hour later the launch whistle sounded at the dock. The three men went down. Frost carried a lantern.

The wooden crate was lashed on deck, and even in the dark they could see the magnificent shape of the silver-white stag through the bars. He had an impressive rack of horns.

McKinzie walked around the crate holding the lantern above his head. He said nothing. The stag turned his head, following him. His big, round, liquid eyes reflected the lantern's glow.

Captain Edwards stroked his mustache and said, "A

right noble animal, Mr. McKinzie. A right noble animal."

"He'll do," McKinzie said. "Let's get the crate on the dock and turn him loose."

It took the four men to wrestle the crate onto the dock. There Captain Edwards unlocked the door and swung it wide. The stag stepped out. He took several dainty, mincing steps, stamped a slender hoof and lifted his head high. His nostrils flared, taking in all the strange scents of the island. Then McKinzie swung the lantern in his face and shouted, "Hah! Hah!" The stag snorted and bolted off the dock into the surrounding brush.

They stood there a minute after it had disappeared; then McKinzie said matter-of-factly, "We'll go after him first thing in the morning." He swung stiffly off the dock and headed for the lodge.

As soon as the sun dropped beneath the horizon and night lay across the forest floor, Paul led Sandy down the rock pile and up the trail to the spring. There Sandy drank his fill, then sat down, wrapped his tail around his feet and began washing his face with one wrist. Paul lay full length and drank. He had almost finished when the chain was ripped from his hand, almost tearing his fingers off. He looked around. Sandy was sailing through the air after a fleeing rabbit.

Paul jumped up and sprinted after him, calling, "Sandy, come back here. Sandy. Sandy."

Sandy was loose for the first time in several days, and there was a live rabbit racing tantalizingly ahead of him. It was too much to resist. He dodged through the trees and brush in hot pursuit, long tail streaming out behind, loose chain snapping and bouncing.

Cat and rabbit disappeared.

Paul kept running, hoping Sandy had caught the rabbit and he'd come upon him eating it. He followed the direction he thought Sandy and the rabbit had taken. He did not find them.

Paul finally came into the trail that led to the lodge. Maybe Sandy had taken it again. He followed it toward the lodge, peering intently into the dark.

The lodge was a blaze of light. He moved carefully closer and made out McKinzie, Frost and Ironwood standing on the porch. He could not hear what they were saying.

Paul waited behind a bush hoping Sandy would not appear. Finally the men went inside. One by one the lights were extinguished. Paul circled the building and went down to the dock. Far out he saw the running lights of a boat. A wooden crate, with an open door, was on the dock. Paul sat on the edge of the dock until the running lights of the boat were swallowed by the night. Sandy did not come. Finally Paul left the dock and walked up the beach calling softly, "Sandy. Here, Sandy. Sandy. Sandy."

Where the beach ran out he stopped and considered his next move. There was no sense rambling around in the dark. The chances of finding Sandy were practically nonexistent. He was a night prowler and could be anywhere. He might as well return to the cave and hope Sandy would come back early. If he just didn't snag the chain and get hung up somewhere. He wondered idly if Sandy had caught the rabbit.

Sandy had not caught the rabbit. The first few jumps he was almost upon it. Then the dragging chain whipped around a clump of brush and momentarily slowed him. The rabbit disappeared. Sandy trotted on. He was happy to be free, doing the one thing that came naturally to his kind—hunting. He raised two more rabbits. Each time the dragging chain hindered him and the rabbits escaped. Fortunately there was no large ring or toggle in the end to catch in the brush and hold him fast. For the most part it slid smoothly over the ground with only momentary snags that easily broke loose. But its passage through the grass made a small rustling that alerted game.

Chasing the rabbits had taken Sandy to the far side of the island. He turned, finally, circled back and came into the main trail to the lodge. At the lodge he walked around the buildings, then went on to the dock. He sniffed about the empty crate, picked up the stag smell and became momentarily excited. But there was nothing there to stalk. He quit the dock and padded along the beach, following the water's edge. Finally he cut back into the timber and began the aimless wandering that always occupied him most of the night.

Sandy raised another rabbit, but all his stealth did him

no good. The rabbit sprinted away and disappeared. A frightened pheasant exploded out of the grass well beyond leaping range and zoomed away. He was frustrated and angry when he came to an open glade. The moon was bright, and in the center of it stood a magnificent silver-white stag.

The deer family has always been a cougar's favorite prey. Sandy instinctively knew this and sank belly-flat. He watched the stag for several minutes, and the ancient excitement of the stalk, the kill, built within him. He waited for the stag to wander toward him. But the animal remained well out in the open, feeding. It lifted its head every few moments to look about.

Sandy could wait no longer. He began his stalk. The grass was several feet high, making it easy for him to hide. At this distance the rustling chain did not disturb the stag.

Sandy moved when the stag's head was down, feeding. He crouched motionless when the animal raised his head. Sandy had never stalked anything larger than the island rabbits. But he went about this as if he'd done it all his life. He managed to creep within half a dozen long jumps. Then some sixth sense warned the animal. The stag jerked his head up and looked about after every bite. He snorted delicately and stamped his front feet.

Sandy lay perfectly still. He knew this animal was very fast. He had to get close enough so his second leap would land him on the stag's back. He moved forward inch by inch, not disturbing a single blade of grass.

The stag walked a small, nervous circle, head high, ready to bound away.

Forty feet off Sandy crouched, long sinuous body at one with the earth. One by one his powerful legs coiled beneath him. The stag lowered his head into the grass. Sandy launched himself silently through the air.

Sandy's second leap should have put him on the stag. But the trailing chain made a fatal rustling through the grass. The stag's head snapped up. He whirled, and in one fluid motion bounded away. Sandy's second leap dropped him into the grass a dozen feet short. He chased the stag across the meadow, but the whipping chain slowed him down. The stag pulled away and disappeared into the surrounding trees.

Sandy stopped, panting, looking after the disappearing stag. Then in complete frustration and anger he raised his head and gave vent to a piercing scream.

Dawn was chasing the night shadows when Sandy returned to the rock pile an climbed to the cave.

Paul awoke when he felt the warm body press against him. He sat up and patted Sandy's head and ran his hand down the sleek body. 'I'm glad you're back, and that you didn't get hung up someplace. Now all we've got to do is lie low until McKinzie leaves and your troubles are almost over. What do you think of that?'' He tied the chain to the stick he'd wedged in the wall, lay down beside the cat and was soon asleep, smiling and satisfied.

Alec Frost was also satisfied. McKinzie had lost his cat but the Persian fallow deer more than made up for it. The lumberman never let anyone know he was pleased. But Frost knew he was. His job was safe.

Frost was about to drop off to sleep when he was jerked wide awake by a high, savage scream that tore through the night silence. He sat bolt upright, listening. The scream did not come again. It didn't matter. There was no mistaking that sound. Amazingly the cat was still here on the island. Excitement bubbled up in Alec Frost. Never had he known such luck. He could hardly wait for morning.

11

McKinzie took the news of Sandy's screaming exactly as Frost knew he would—with no show of emotion. But Frost recognized that certain expression in his dark eyes that the gamekeeper had come to call the predatory look.

"You're sure about that?" McKinzie asked. "You heard the cat? You didn't dream it?"

"I heard him, Mr. McKinzie. I've heard that cat a dozen times in the past." Ironwood came into the room and Frost added, "So has Joe. That right, Joe?"

"In the past, yes," Ironwood said. "Why?"

"I heard him last night." Frost couldn't keep the excitement out of his voice. "I'd gone to bed and was just lying there when I heard him. He's still here on the island. That scream sounded mighty healthy."

"Could have been wind whistling in the eaves," Ironwood suggested. "It makes a kind of screaming sound."

"There was no wind last night. You know that."

"We've been hearing loons lately. It could have been a loon. Loon could sound like a cat, if a man heard it when he was half asleep."

"I wasn't half asleep. I was wide awake. I know the cry of a loon as well as you do. I tell you I heard that cat. You trying to make a liar out of me, Joe?" Frost was angry.

Ironwood shook his head. "Just trying to make sense. If you heard him, then where's he been these last days? Mr. McKinzie's combed this island from end to end and hasn't seen a sign of him. This island's not so big an animal like that cougar could hide as long as this without leaving a trace or sign of some kind. You saw him every day. I saw him a number of times. Why hasn't Mr. McKinzie? Then we put out baits. If he's on the island why didn't that rooster bring him? You can hear him all over? I say he's gone. You heard something else."

"You tell me what I heard, Joe," Frost challenged. "What animal or bird screams exactly like a cougar? I'll tell you. Nothing. I don't know where that cat's been hiding, or how Mr. McKinzie missed him, or why our baits didn't work. I do know there's holes and protected spots where he could lay up. That's exactly what I think he's done. I know what I heard. He's here. I'll bet my life on it."

"All right," McKinzie said, "we'll say he's here. How do you figure to find him when I couldn't?"

Frost had known McKinzie would ask that question,

and he'd worked out an answer. "You got all the other animals by walking the trails. Eventually they showed up on one, or near one, and you bagged them. It hasn't worked with this cat because he hasn't hung around the trails, at least not in daylight. This cat's smart. He's been hiding out during the day in a hole, or ravine, or brush patch completely away from the beaten paths. You've got to get off the trails, or know where these hiding places are. I'll go with you today and show them to you. I'm betting we find him. I know this island like the palm of my hand."

"All right," McKinzie agreed. "But no gun for you. I do the shooting. I can't put an animal that I haven't killed in my trophy room."

"Of course, Mr. McKinzie."

"Why not get the deer first?" Ironwood suggested, playing for time to slip away and warn Paul of this new development. "The cat could get the deer before you find him. Then you'd lose your rare deer. By taking the deer first you're sure of getting both."

McKinzie shook his head. "This cat's caused me plenty of trouble. To me he's still number one. I'll chance it losing the deer. We go after the cat this morning. As soon as we get him we start looking for the deer. Another thing," he said to Frost, "the first place we look is that cave. Shooting into it never did satisfy me. That's a perfect place for a cat to hide out. This morning we check it out thoroughly."

"Whatever you say," Frost agreed.

"Then let's get going."

Ironwood waited until Frost and McKinzie disappeared down the trail; then he took off running through the trees. He, too, was headed for the rock pile. His way was much longer, but by hurrying he hoped to get there ahead of them and get Paul and Sandy out of the cave.

During the months he'd walked the trails, keeping them clear for McKinzie, Ironwood hadn't realized how tough the undergrowth was to get through. The ground, down logs, rocks, and stumps were blanketed with slick moss. Trailing vines, protruding roots sent him sprawling. Ravines and low spots were soggy and he sank to his shoe tops. Spines of devil's club snagged his clothing and stung his face and hands.

When he reached the edge of the little glade, sobbing for breath, McKinzie and Frost stood there looking up at the cave entrance.

Frost asked, surprised, "Joe, what're you doing here?"

Ironwood gave him the only answer he could find at the moment: "I got to thinking, if Mr. McKinzie kills the cougar you'll need help carrying him in. And I guess I'm just curious to see if he's up there. I've—I've seen that cave entrance."

McKinzie gave Ironwood an annoyed glance, then returned his attention to the cave. "That's got to be about the best place on the island for a cat to lay up. I'm going up there for a look."

"Shoot into the cave first, Mr. McKinzie," Frost suggested. "It could save quite a climb. If he's in there

144

he'll come flying out. That cat's scared to death of a rifle. Ask Joe. He's seen him take off like an arrow when I shot close."

"That's right," Ironwood agreed. "The sound of a gun scares him plenty. If he's there you can bet he'll come charging out."

McKinzie nodded. He lifted the rifle. The crash of the shot went smashing across the island. He jacked a fresh shell into the barrel and waited. A flock of crows flapped noisily away. The small life about them was hushed.

Ironwood held his breath. Any moment there might be noise from there, or Paul or the cat might appear.

There was nothing.

McKinzie shot again. Again they waited. Nothing happened at the mouth of the cave. A crow began scolding. A squirrel chattered from a limb. "That settles it," McKinzie said. "I've wanted to look inside that cave ever since I started this hunt. Now I'm going to."

"I'll go up. It won't take but a couple of minutes." Ironwood started across the glade.

"Hold it." McKinzie's voice was sharp. "I said I'm going. So it'll take a little longer. I want to see inside that cave with my own eyes."

"I thought I could save you time," Ironwood explained.

"I'm here. I'll take the time. You fellows wait."

Ironwood stood with Alec Frost and watched the lumberman swing stiffly across the glade and slowly begin to climb.

145

The smash of McKinzie's first shot jerked Paul out of a sound sleep. Sandy was on his feet straining at the end of the chain. Paul threw both arms around his neck and forced him down, whispering, "No. Lie down, Sandy. Lie down. Stay, Sandy! Stay!" Under his hands and urging voice, Sandy sank back to the floor, trembling violently. Paul held him and waited for another shot. It came, and at the back of the cave a rock exploded into dust. The sound rolled up in diminishing waves. Again it was all Paul could do to hold the cat. There were no more shots. In a few moments Sandy became quiet again.

Paul crept to the mouth of the cave, rose to hands and knees and peeked down into the glade. He saw Ironwood and Frost looking at the rock pile. But their attention was not focused as high as the cave. He leaned out a little further, and peered down through the notch in the ledge. McKinzie came into view, climbing slowly toward the mouth of the cave. He had slung the rifle across his shoulder by the strap and was working his way carefully from rock to rock.

Paul slid back down to Sandy. They were trapped. McKinzie was going to get Sandy at last. What had gone wrong? The lumberman was supposed to have left the island. His mind raced, seeking a way out. He was surprised how cool his thinking was. Maybe these days of tension had prepared him for this.

He could step outside in plain sight. That would stop McKinzie, but only temporarily. He could turn Sandy loose and let him charge out of the cave. He might get away for the moment. McKinzie would know he was here and could take his time tracking the cat down. He'd spent days trying to save Sandy from this man who only wanted to kill him so he could brag about it. Anger welled up in him at the climbing, relentless McKinzie. If Sandy was cornered, so was he. Sandy was his responsibility. Sandy depended upon him for protection. Big and strong as he was, he was frightened and helpless.

Paul looked quickly about the cave for some kind of weapon. His eyes lit on the four-foot length of limb wedged into the crack in the rock to hold Sandy's chain. He untied the chain, pulled the limb out of the crack and hefted it. It was heavy. It was a weapon.

Paul crept to the mouth of the cave and peeked through the crevice. McKinzie was climbing slowly, carefully, placing his stiff leg with great care. He was only a couple of minutes below the cave ledge. If the man glanced up at the crevice, he'd see him. Paul slid back down the incline. He tried to think. There was nothing left to think about.

The days he hid like an animal, ducked through the trees to avoid being seen, lived on the little that Ironwood sneaked to him—all to save Sandy—came down to this one second in time. Everything that had happened from the moment he ran away from the motel in Seattle pointed to this showdown. Sandy would be killed, or he fought with anything, and in any way he

147

could. He gripped the club. He was going to fight.

The first thing Paul saw was the muzzle of the rifle McKinzie had slung over his shoulder. Then his head came slowly into view. Paul remembered that the last couple of feet, McKinzie would have to turn sideways for foot- and hand-holds. When he stood on top he would be turned sideways to the cave entrance. He could not look inside until he made that half turn.

Paul could hear McKinzie's bellowslike breathing, the grunting sounds as he laboriously pulled himself upward. Then he was standing on top, unslinging the rifle, starting to turn to look inside.

Paul gripped the club and rose. Some cool part of his mind said, "Now! Before he sees you!" He charged up the incline swinging the club.

McKinzie heard him coming and whirled. He tried to bring the rifle to bear. The foot of his stiff leg came down on a round rock. It rolled and destroyed his balance. He stumbled back, fighting to stay upright. The stiff leg refused to move. He went over backward off the ledge. One moment his startled eyes looked straight into Paul's. His mouth was sprung wide in a silent scream, his arms outflung. The rifle sailed into the air. Then he dropped down from sight.

There was a thunderous explosion of the rifle, a startled yell and a soft thud.

Sandy shot out of the cave mouth and disappeared.

Paul ran to the lip of the ledge and looked down. Thirty feet below, the still form of George McKinzie was wedged between two big rocks. Ironwood and Frost were scrambling frantically up the rocks to McKinzie. Had they looked as high as the cave, they'd have seen him.

Paul watched the two men carry the unconscious, or maybe dead, McKinzie down to the floor of the glade and there fashion a stretcher of his jacket and a pair of poles. Then they carried him down the trail toward the lodge.

Paul stood there uncertainly, looking down at the empty glade. Then he turned back inside. He still carried the club and dropped it on the floor. He felt shaky. His legs were weak. He sat down and leaned against the wall and reached deep for breath. His heart hammered painfully. He wondered where Sandy was, then remembered he was dragging the chain.

Paul was glad he hadn't hit McKinzie. He'd probably have knocked him off the ledge. But what had brought McKinzie up here? He was supposed to leave today, convinced Sandy was gone. Now they knew he wasn't. To make matters worse, McKinzie had seen him as he fell. Everything that had been going so well had turned sour. He was at a loss what to do now.

Paul decided to stay in the cave and await Sandy's return, wait for Ironwood to come and tell him what had happened to McKinzie and what he should do now. He made a sandwich, but was too nervous to eat and put it aside. For some reason he felt cold in the cave. He went outside, sat down on the ledge in the sun and tried not to

149

think what the morning's happenings might mean. Somehow everything seemed to depend on Ironwood now.

His shaking gradually subsided and he became calm again. The sun climbed the sky. The day turned warm. A small breeze whispered through the trees, rustling the leaves. The scent of fir and the earth and the distant sea seemed particularly strong this morning.

He didn't hear Sandy come. But suddenly he was rubbing against his shoulder and purring contentedly as if nothing had happened. "Wish I could forget like you." Paul patted his head. "I'm glad you're back. But maybe you shouldn't have come, or maybe you should. I don't know anymore."

Sandy lay down close beside him, put a paw over his eyes and went to sleep.

Together they waited for Ironwood.

The sun had dropped behind the curtain of trees and the first long shadows patterned the little glade when Ironwood climbed the rock pile and sat down beside him. He looked tired.

"Been quite a day," he said. "I figured you'd be in the cave. You know what happened?"

"I know," Paul said. "How is Mr. McKinzie?"

"We had him in the hospital in less than two hours. Frost called a helicopter rescue crew by shortwave. They flew out and picked up all three of us. He's unconscious, got a concussion. His hip's broke on the stiff leg

150

side and he has some broken ribs. The doctor says
there's no reason he shouldn't recover. But his hunting
days are over. He'll be on crutches from now on."

"I'm sorry," Paul said. "He shouldn't have tried to
climb up here. What happened anyway? You told me he
was leaving."

Ironwood told him about the stag and Frost hearing
Sandy scream. "Did you turn him loose last night?"

"He got away." Paul told him what happened at the
spring. "He came back this morning."

Ironwood shook his head tiredly. "I guess things took
a turn for the better a little too fast. The fat's really in
the fire now. Frost saw Sandy run out of the cave, jump
McKinzie, and knock him off the ledge."

"He didn't."

"You can't protect him this time, Paul. I saw it."

"From where you were on the ground I guess it
looked like Sandy jumped him. But he didn't." Paul
explained what happened. "You see," he finished, "I
was the one who caused him to fall."

"You hit him with the club?"

"I didn't even get close to him. The round rock under
his foot made him lose his balance and he fell."

"Neither of us saw you," Ironwood said. "All we
saw was McKinzie falling and Sandy bounding away."

"What caused the shot?"

"When the rifle hit the rocks below, it discharged.
Anyway, it's too bad. Frost thinks Sandy knocked him
off that ledge."

"What difference does it make? He fell, that's all."

"It makes all the difference. This gamekeeper job is the best Frost has ever had. He loves it. Now that McKinzie will never hunt again, the lodge will be closed up and the island sold. That's the end of Frost's plush job. Naturally he blames Sandy for losing it. He's a vengeful man. He's going to kill Sandy to get even if it's the last thing he does."

"McKinzie won't stand for it. Sandy's his trophy."

"Sandy will never be his trophy now. In his present condition he couldn't care less what Frost does."

"Then I'll buy Sandy from Frost. Nobody ever need know the difference."

"You don't reason with a man as mad as Alec Frost. Killing Sandy is the only thing that will satisfy him."

"What can we do?"

"That's what I've come to tell you. Not a thing, Paul. This is the end of the line."

"I don't understand."

"You can't do anything more to save Sandy, and neither can I. Frost is bringing in dogs to hunt Sandy down. They'll be here by launch tonight. Tomorrow morning they'll track Sandy down and Frost will kill him."

"No. There must be something we can do. Something . . ."

Ironwood shook his head. "There's not a cave, crevice or tree where those dogs won't find him. They're trained hunting dogs. You might as well come into the

152

lodge with me and let Frost send you back to your folks. You can always know you did your best. And believe me, it's a lot more than anyone I've ever known would do.''

Paul kept shaking his head. ''Leave Sandy out here to face Frost and those dogs alone after all we've been through together? I won't desert him now.''

''You still don't get the picture,'' Ironwood said patiently. ''They're coming after Sandy tomorrow with dogs that follow a scent. Wherever Sandy leaves a paw scent on this island they'll find it and run him down. And Frost will be right behind them with the rifle. Can't you understand that?''

''I understand,'' Paul said stubbornly. ''When they run Sandy down I'll be there, too.''

''Frost won't hurt you. But your being there won't stop him from killing Sandy.''

''Maybe not. But I have to be there.''

''What do you think you can do?''

''I don't know. I thought McKinzie would kill him this morning but he didn't. Something could happen tomorrow, too. I've come this far with Sandy. I can't quit now. I've got to keep trying as long as Sandy's alive. I don't want to be there at the end. I didn't want to face McKinzie with just a stick this morning. I'll have to do anything I can tomorrow. You can understand that.''

Ironwood's black eyes studied him a long moment. ''I guess you're right. I should have known what you'd do. I admit I'm tempted to tell Frost about you and let him call the police to come pick you up. But I can't do a thing like that to somebody who's shown as much fight and courage as you have. You've earned the right to do what you want to. I intend to respect that right.

"One thing I will promise you. I'll be with Frost tomorrow. If there's any way I can help you I will. Just one bit of advice: don't let Frost and the dogs corner you in the cave. Get out early. Head for the far end of the island. Walk in water. It'll throw the dogs off the scent. They'll have to hunt for it and you'll gain time. Double back on your track. Walk a log, go over rocks, wade in a stream or in the ocean. Do everything you can think of to confuse them. And above all, keep your eyes open for anything, anything at all that will help you. That's about all I can tell you. It's not much."

"I'll do the best I can."

"I know you will. I hate to leave you like this, but I'm fresh out of ideas. I'm at the end of my rope. You are, too, but you don't know it. Maybe that's the way it should be." He rose and stood looking down at Paul thoughtfully. "Every time I hear you sing, I'll remember how you fooled old Limpy McKinzie and Alec Frost for a week."

"With your help," Paul said.

"A little, maybe." Ironwood held out his hand. "If I don't see you again, the pleasure has been mine."

For the first time in his life, Paul felt he was shaking hands man to man.

He watched the bandy-legged little Indian climb down the rock face and disappear. For some strange reason he felt good in spite of the terrible obstacle that lay ahead tomorrow. He wished he had some idea what it would be like. Somehow, he told himself sternly, he would meet it as he'd met the other problems since he came here: head on.

12

For all his brave resolve, Paul could not sleep. He should have been hungry since he'd not eaten all day. But the sandwich he tried to eat seemed to stick in his throat. He took out the last of the meat and fed it to Sandy. Sandy ate it, then paced nervously back and forth and looked longingly out the cave entrance at the inviting night. Finally he settled down and went to sleep.

Paul worried through the long, dark hours. He tried to think of some way they could escape from the island, some place they could hide where the dogs wouldn't find them. There was none. He tried to form some plan of what he should do if the dogs and Frost cornered them somewhere. He couldn't plan because he didn't know how, or where, or even if they might be cornered or what the circumstances might be.

Ironwood had said he'd be with Frost and would try to help them. Paul didn't need the help, Frost wouldn't harm him, and the little Indian had admitted there was nothing he could do for Sandy. Then he realized how right Ironwood was when he said, "This is the end of the line. Nothing can be done." Sandy and he could do only one thing, run in circles around the island until Frost and the dogs cornered them. Since that was what it came down to, Paul told himself, they'd begin running plenty early. They'd give Frost and the dogs all the run they could, right up to the end. What he'd do then, he hadn't the faintest idea.

When dawn cut the dark under the trees enough to see to travel, Paul untied the chain from the wedged stick and woke Sandy. They went down the face of the rock pile and headed for the far end of the island.

The sun finally chased the last of the shadows, and the day stood bright and clear. A covey of quail scattered through the long grass, calling back and forth to each other. A rabbit surveyed them, chewing industriously on a stem of sweet grass. Crows sat thick in a small tree, silent for once as they passed. In the distance the faint talking of gulls barely disturbed the silence. It didn't seem possible that a man with a rifle and hunting dogs could be after them on such a perfect morning.

Paul remembered Ironwood's instructions for confusing the dogs. He came to a shallow stream, pulled Sandy into the water and splashed down it for some distance. Sandy did not like the water. He splashed along daintily, lifting big paws high and frowning distastefully.

157

They quit the stream in the thickest patch of brush Paul could find. Sandy shook each paw and wanted to sit down and wash his face. Paul yanked on the chain. "Not now," he said. "Come on. We've got to keep moving."

Paul found a down log, got Sandy to climb on top, and they walked the length of it, jumped across to another and doubled back. They waded a second stream, came to a small, marshy lake, splashed ankle-deep halfway around that body of water and climbed a rocky bank.

The sun was well up. The first heat of the day beat down on them. Sweat was streaking Paul's face and stinging his eyes when they came out on the beach. He led Sandy into the shallow water and they waded parallel to the beach until they reached a low spine of rock that protruded into the sea. They climbed over the rock and entered the sea again and continued on until brush grew right down into the water and forced them back to the land.

They cut inland for a distance, then backtracked and hiked over the most unlikely, rugged places along the edge of a steep ravine. They fought their way through a tangle of briars and devil's club that stung every part of the skin it touched.

Sandy objected to much of this and hung back. Paul yanked on the chain and constantly talked to him, sometimes coaxing, sometimes threatening. "Come on, we're going to make this as tough for them as we can. I'm trying to save your life. You just remember that."

And because he'd been so well trained, the big cat padded along beside him.

They came to the beach again and began wading in ankle-deep water. Paul judged they had completely crossed and circled about half the island. Considering the distance they'd traveled and all the diversionary tactics they'd employed to throw the dogs off the scent, he didn't see how they could possibly be followed.

They were wading a shallow tide pool when Paul heard the first sound. He stopped dead in the water and listened. It came again, clear, unmistakable, riding the quiet morning like the voices of doom. The excited baying of a pair of hounds. It was far off, but Paul could visualize them coming fast. They were apparently unraveling with ease the intricate trail Sandy and he had taken so much time to weave.

The voices stopped abruptly. They had lost the trail. Paul waited, holding his breath. In a minute the baying started up again, sharp, excited. It hadn't taken them long to sniff out the trail. A ball of fear settled in the pit of his stomach. His palms were wet. Then he was angry. What right did those dogs have to chase them? He'd like to kill them both.

Paul began running through the shallow water, dragging Sandy. Sandy hung back, annoyed at this sudden change of speed. Paul yanked hard on the chain. "Come on, you darned fool," he almost yelled. "We've got to get out of here. Come on!"

Sandy finally fell in beside him and loped along easily.

Paul turned directly away from the sounds of the dogs. Soon they ran out of shallow water where a rocky point jutted into the sea, and once again Paul took to the brush. He had no idea where he was going. He meant to stay ahead of those dogs as long as he could.

He stopped often to listen. The dogs were gaining at an alarming pace. He continued to try to confuse them by backtracking on their trail and walking through water. But nothing helped. He quit trying to confuse the dogs, because it was only slowing him up, and simply ran straight away at top speed. Sandy stayed close beside him.

They raced into a wide, open meadow. On the far side was a thick screen of brush and trees. Beyond that, once again, was the sea. Paul had no idea what he'd do, or what they might find once they reached the beach.

They tore through the screen of trees and brush and were on the beach. Paul stopped, panting, and looked about. A sharp point of brush-covered rocks extened several hundred feet out to sea. Except for that there was no place to run except along the smooth, open beach. In either direction it was a long way to sheltering brush or trees. The dogs and Frost would see them the moment they came through the brush screen.

Paul listened to the voices of the dogs. They were clear and sharp and very close. They weren't far from the open meadow.

For the first time Sandy showed concern. His head turned, his ears came forward, his yellow eyes searched the screen of brush. His lips lifted in a snarl. No matter

160

what direction they went, they were trapped right here against the sea. Paul bent and picked up a rock and hefted it in his hand. He had been prepared to fight McKinzie with a club. He'd fight these dogs and Frost with rocks.

Then he saw something the tall brush at the point of land had hidden. His moving to pick up the rock had brought it into view. A white fishing boat, with poles on top of the cabin, was riding at anchor about a hundred feet off the point. He guessed it was about thirty feet long. There was no one on deck.

His mind began racing. If they could get aboard that boat there was a possible escape. Maybe the fisherman had pulled in to sleep or repair his motor. He could call to him and the man could row in and pick them up in that little rowboat he was towing astern. Then he remembered Sandy. No stranger was going to come in to pick up a full-grown cougar. He'd have to explain the situation and that Sandy was tame. There was no time for that. They had to get on that boat immediately, before the dogs broke through the screen of brush and saw them, and before the fisherman was aware of them and could raise objections or panic.

It was an easy swim for Paul. He didn't know about Sandy. He had waded into the sea his first night here, but would he swim? There was one way to find out. Paul started toward the point, then stopped. If they entered at the point, the dogs would find their scent there, and Frost would know they had sum to the boat. They had to enter the sea here, on the main beach, wade to

161

the point and then begin swimming. That way, he hoped, Frost would be left right here, to guess which way they'd gone.

Paul took an extra wrap of the chain around his hand and said, "Come on, Sandy. Come on. Hurry up." He waded into the water and Sandy dutifully followed, stepping daintily, his face plainly showing distaste.

They splashed to the very point of land and now Paul heard the voices of the dogs above the noise Sandy and he were making. They must be crossing the open meadow.

Paul waded to his chest, prepared to begin swimming, and there with just his head out of water, Sandy balked. Paul yanked savagely on the chain. "Come!" he said angrily. "Come on! They're almost here. Come on, Sandy!" He leaned backward and pulled with all his strength. Sandy stretched his head out and suddenly began to swim.

Sandy was a good swimmer. His big, wide paws drove him through the water at a speed Paul, for all his practice, could not equal. Sandy headed straight for the one thing that offered something solid to climb onto. The boat.

There was a low projection across the stern, like a step. Sandy scrambled onto that and into the boat with Paul right behind him. They had crawled aboard at one side of the boat, and their combined weight caused it to rock sharply.

Almost immediately a tall, thin man in undershirt and pants emerged from the cabin rubbing sleep from his eyes and grumbling, "What the devil's going on?" He saw Sandy. His pale blue eyes flew wide. His mouth fell open. He backed against the cabin door holding his hands out as if to ward off an attack and mumbling in a frightened voice, "No! No! Oh, my god! No!

Paul kept a close grip on Sandy's chain and said, "Relax, mister. Listen to me."

The fisherman kept muttering, "No, no! Get him out of here. Get him out!"

Paul knew he had to get through to this man immediately or the dogs would burst onto the beach and see them here on deck. He said sharply, "I said listen, mister. Pay attention to me if you want to live. You hear me?"

"What?" The fisherman couldn't take his terrified eyes off Sandy. The cat's mouth was open, panting from the exertion of the swim and running. To the fisherman, still half asleep, Sandy was snarling, about to leap upon him. "Wh-what's that you say? What's that?"

Paul made his voice tough. "This cougar will do whatever I say. You're perfectly safe just as long as you do exactly as I tell you. Do you understand?"

"Yeah, sure. Sure." The fisherman began to get hold of himself. "Just hang on to that cat. Don't let him go, boy."

"I won't," Paul said, "if you listen."

"I'm listening, boy."

Paul jerked his head toward the beach and the sounds of the approaching dogs, which he could tell were now working their way through the fringe of the trees. "Hear that? Those dogs, and a man with a rifle, are chasing us. They want to kill this cat. I'm not going to let them and you're going to help me."

"Anything you say. I don't argue with a cougar. What do I do?"

"You stand up here in the stern, in plain sight where they can see you. If they ask you if you've seen us, you're going to tell them you haven't. This cat and I will be right in your cabin with the door open, watching you signal that man, or give us away in any manner, and I'll turn the cat loose on you. Just remember, no matter what happens to him or me, he'll get you first. Do you understand that?"

"Sure, boy, sure," the fisherman said hastily. "Anything you say. Just hang on to that cat."

"I will," Paul said, "as long as you do as you're told. We're going into the cabin now. Remember, I'll be watching."

Paul had barely gotten Sandy into the cabin and closed the door to a crack when two black hounds burst through the brush onto the beach. They ran straight to the spot where Sandy and he entered the water, stopped and began to bark excitedly. They stayed there and continued to bark until Frost and Ironwood stepped from the brush a few minutes later.

Frost carried a rifle in the crook of his arm. He walked to the spot where the dogs waited and looked about. Then he called to the fisherman, "Hey, did you see a cougar running along the shore here?"

164

"Cougar!" The fisherman shook his head. "Been no cougars on this island in years. Ain't nothing much left but rabbits and squirrels since you fellers came out here."

"There's a cougar here now," Frost said. "The dogs trailed him to here." He pointed at the spot Paul and Sandy entered the water. "I thought you might have seen him."

"I've been asleep. Had a long day yesterday," the fisherman explained. "Your dogs' barking woke me. I just came on deck to see what was up. A cougar, you say. Maybe your cat walked in the water to hide his tracks. Other animals do."

"Cougar's ain't generally that smart," Frost said.

"This one is. We know that," Ironwood put in. "He's been doing it all morning, plus doubling back on his trail. We'll have to go both ways along the beach until the dogs pick up his scent again."

Frost fiddled with the bolt on the rifle and kept scowling at the boat. "It just don't seem right—a cat as smart as this one—and him entering the water right at this spot. It seems mighty odd to me."

"Nothing odd about it," Ironwood explained. "The cat broke out of the brush right here and ran out of land. He had to enter the water to go either direction. This just happened to be the spot he did it. Nothing surprising or odd about that. The boat and the fisherman have nothing to do with it. He was taking a nap where it was nice and quiet till we showed up."

"I suppose so," Frost finally grumbled. "Still it

165

seems kind of funny. Guess we might as well head up the beach and see if we can raise him again." He started off, the dogs racing ahead of him.

Ironwood stood there looking at the boat. He saw the wet transom where Sandy and Paul had crawled on board. He began to smile. He lifted a hand, still smiling, then turned and followed Frost.

The fisherman said, "All right, boy. They're gone. Now what?"

"Stay there until I tell you to come in here."

Paul waited until Frost and the dogs were almost out of sight. Then he said, "All right, come in here where I can talk to you."

"I can hear you fine from here."

"You don't have to worry about Sandy," Paul said. "He's tame."

"Oh, sure." The fisherman was getting back a little courage. "You know it and I know it, but does he know it?"

"I'm with him," Paul pointed out. "I have been for more than a week. I tell you there's nothing to be afraid of."

The fisherman edged inside and stood uncertainly inside the door. Sandy glanced at him, then lifted a paw, licked his wrist and began washing his face. "What's so important about me being in here instead of on deck?" the fisherman asked.

"Frost, the man with the rifle, was suspicious. He might double back for a second look. He could tell if you were talking to somebody inside."

"You're pretty smart." The fisherman sat down carefully on the edge of the bunk. "All right, what do you want from me?"

"Do you know where Skull Island is?"

The fisherman nodded. "About twenty miles further out to sea. It used to be an Indian burial ground. There's nothing there."

"Can you take us out there?"

"Yeah, I can. But like I said, there's nothing there. No houses, no people. Nothing."

"That's what I want. I'll pay you."

"This don't look good to me," the fisherman said. "A kid running around with the biggest cougar I've ever seen, being chased by a man with dogs, now wanting to go out to Skull, and offering to pay, like hiring a boat was nothing. Cougar or no, I want to know what this is all about. It sounds to me like I could be getting in big trouble with the law and maybe even lose my boat."

"Let's get away from this island," Paul said, "and I'll tell you everything."

"Good enough." The fisherman went forward, pulled up the anchor and returned. "You hold that cat so I can get to the wheel."

Paul held Sandy close. The fisherman eased carefully past and slipped into the seat behind the wheel. A moment later the motor started. They began moving out to sea. Paul heaved a sigh of relief.

They traveled until the island was no more than a dot on the sea; then the fisherman shut off the motor and they drifted. He turned in the seat and said, "All right, let's have it, boy. I've seen some strange things in twenty years' fishing, but nothing like this.''

As he had with Ironside, Paul began with the day he'd run away and told it all right down to when Sandy and he swam out to the boat. The fisherman listened and kept shaking his head in amazement.

When he finished the fisherman said, ''That's the darnedest story I've ever heard. It's mighty hard to believe, but I do. So you're the lost singer kid that disappeared. I did hear about it, but not much. Except for going in for supplies and to deliver fish, I've been at sea almost constantly the past month. You get pretty well out of contact with what's going on in the world. And this cat, this Sandy. . . . He's that TV cat I've seen so often on the screen. How about that. And now you want to go out to Skull Island. Why Skull?''

''I want to turn him loose where he can live without somebody hunting him. Joe Ironwood said it was a good place.''

''The best. Big, lots of game. No people.''

''If you'll take us out and then bring me back, I'll pay you.''

The fisherman smiled and rubbed his chin. ''Tell you what, Paul. That is your name, right? I'll take you out and bring you back and it won't cost a dime. That Frost, and especially McKinzie, are no friends of mine, or of anybody else that lives around here. We don't like what he's doing one little bit. Besides that, McKinzie and his friends are mighty reckless with their shooting. They've almost hit a couple of local boats, and somebody did hit mine. Knocked slivers out of the bow. I'm glad for the chance to take a crack at those people. By the way, my name's Watson, Hank Watson.'' He leaned forward studying Sandy. "I've never been this close to a cougar before.''

"You can pet him," Paul said.

"You're sure? He won't claw or bite?''

"He's very tame. Go ahead.''

Watson reached out a hand and gingerly patted Sandy between the ears. Sandy lifted his head, closed his eyes and began to purr. Watson patted harder. He rubbed Sandy's ears and began to smile. "Son of a gun! What do you know!" He laughed outright. "You're all right, Sandy. Yes, sir, you're all right.'' He straightened abruptly. "What say we get moving. It'll be dark when we get back.''

It was the middle of the afternoon when they reached Skull Island. Skull Island was long, with a rocky shoreline and a great stand of timber. They dropped anchor a hundred yards offshore and Watson said, "You and Sandy can go ashore in the dinghy.''

"Dinghy?" Paul asked.

"The little rowboat we've been towing.''

Watson pulled the dinghy alongside, and Paul and Sandy got in. Paul set the oars in the oarlocks and Watson pushed the boat off. I'll wait," he said.

Sandy sat quietly at Paul's feet while he rowed ashore. When they grounded, Paul pulled the dinghy up on the beach, and with Sandy beside him he walked up

169

to the fringe of trees. There Paul unfastened the collar and dropped it on the ground. "Here you are," he said. "This is what all the running around and hiding on the island was about. Maybe it's a good thing you don't understand."

Sandy lifted his head. The white butterfly patch under his nose twitched as he sucked in all the scents of the island. His stubby ears came erect and his yellow eyes looked into the shadows under the trees.

Paul patted his head. His mouth felt dry. His throat ached. "Go ahead," he said softly, "it's all yours for as long as you live. I hope that's a long long time."

Paul turned suddenly and ran back to the boat and dragged it into the water. He pulled hard a couple of times before he looked up. Sandy was standing, looking at him. Then he turned his head and looked into the trees. Paul could see the black tip of his tail curl gently—as if he were waving good-bye. Then he was gone.

They were hours running back. Paul stood by the cabin window and had little to say.

It was dark when they pulled in to a little dock. Watson said. "Maybe you'd better sleep on board till morning. It's about four miles to the nearest settlement."

"I'll be fine. I'm anxious to get back. I'd like to pay you."

Watson shook his head. "My pleasure. It was one chance to take a crack at that McKinzie and his kind."

They shook hands. Watson said, "The road up there

will take you into the settlement where you can get a phone and call your folks.''

The road was narrow. It turned and twisted through a dark forest. Paul wondered if he'd ever see Joe Ironwood again. Probably not. He couldn't have done it without the little Indian's help. But Joe had been wrong about one thing—the Apache legend. The cougar had screamed but no one died. Then he thought of the days he'd spent out there, the things that had happened. He had certainly changed. The Paul Winters who had run away eleven days ago was gone. He was as gone as if he were dead. Maybe the Apache legend was true after all.

Headlights probed the night. A car pulled up beside him. He saw the red and blue lights of a state police car on the roof. The officer leaned out the window and said, ''You're quite a way from town, son. Can I give you a lift or anything?''

Paul stepped to the car and looked in at the officer. ''Yes, sir,'' he said. ''I think you're looking for me.''